Jenny's Way

A Local Legend

By Diana K. Perkins

Copyright © 2012 by Diana K. Perkins
1st Edition – December 2012
ISBN
978-1-77097-857-7 (Hardcover)
978-1-77097-858-4 (Paperback)
978-1-77097-859-1 (eBook)

All rights reserved
This is a fictional novel. Any resemblance to actual lives or persons is purely accidental and should not be taken as fact. Although this novel is set in Baltic, Connecticut, and written about a local legend, the story is fictional. The sections about St. Joseph's school, church and convent are not based upon any school or church in Baltic, Connecticut.

No part of this publication may be reproduced in any form, or by any means, electronic or mechanical, including photocopying, recording, or any information browsing, storage, or retrieval system, without the permission in writing from the publisher.

Author's Notes:
This novel includes an idealized portrayal of sex workers in a small-town bordello. It is not intended to glamorize or minimize the role of these women.

Research shows that eleven cottages, built by villagers as weekend getaways, once stood on the shores of a small lake created by a mill dam on the Shetucket River in Baltic, Connecticut. Legend has it that at one point women may have lived in some of these cottages and "entertained" mill boys there, although no firm evidence of this has been found. The real road to the camp was called Ginny's Lane and descended from the farm on Pautipaug Hill Road in Baltic, not far out of town. The dam, pictured on the postcard above, was just upriver from the bridge on the current Route 97. Today only a few large berms mark its former location, but the Veterans Memorial still exists on the south side of the river where the boardinghouse and men's club once stood.

Produced by:
FriesenPress
Suite 300— 852 Fort Street, Victoria, BC, Canada V8W 1H8
www.friesenpress.com
Distributed to the trade by The Ingram Book Company.

Author's Website: http://dianakperkins.com

Acknowledgements

I want to thank my faithful readers who helped and supported me in bringing this novel to fruition: Barbara Doak, Ellie Maher, Donna Martell, Christine Pattee, Kathy Powers, and especially Eve Brehenne, who continues to direct my feeble attempts at writing with gentle encouragement. Thank you to Laura Lawrence and Terry Cote, whose insightful observations made this a much better story. Thank you to Blanche Boucher, whose clear and concise editing made this a much easier read – what would I have done without you?

Many thanks to my conscientious Friesen Press account manager Sabrina Ali, whose persistence helped to keep me on schedule. A world of thanks goes to the dedicated staff of Friesen Press, which is the best indie press. Thank you to friends who always offer support and encouragement; the list is long and my memory short, but among them are Cheryl Gagne, Loretta and Sharon, Susan and Laurina, the Jennifers, Winky, Valentin, and of course my family.

Thank you to the Ostens, who helped me with research, and to Gary, on whose property the camps stood and who gave me permission to walk on and photograph the site. A sincere thank you to Mary Delaney and Reg Patchell, who spent time going through archives for me, and Judy Synnett and Roy D. Hoffman, all of the Sprague Historical Society. A nod goes out to the librarians at the Sprague Public Library, who have given me kind encouragement.

And a special thank you to my dear Michelle, who suffered through my re-reads and edits and late-night agonies over the computer and printer.

Dedicated to

Frances,

Dorothy,

myself,

and

bad girls

everywhere.

This is a tribute to small towns,

but mostly a tribute to our resilient selves.

Prologue

The Long Look Back

My memory fades now, goes in and out, and I'm sure time and distance color it.

But I remember distinctly the difficult times, and the happy times – those seem burned in like a brand. For those times that are indistinct and out of focus, I have sought the help of my family and friends, Rachael, Emma and Sharon, who have helped me in reaching back.

This is what we remember.

- John E.

Jenny's Way Cottages

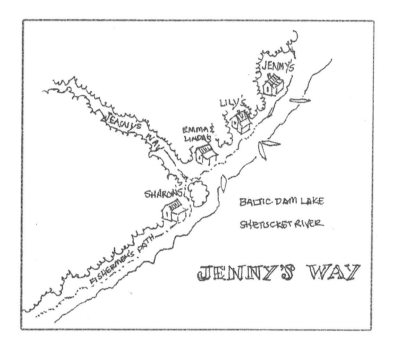

Jenny's Way

Part 1

Chapter 1

Meet John E.

I don't know that we ever see life-changing events for what they are until they've long passed. Often we see only in hindsight those events that forever change our circumstances. We replay them in our minds and wonder whether, if we had reacted differently, the outcome would have sent us down a wholly different path. We try to imagine another life, maybe a better life but possibly worse.

I could not have guessed that Friday afternoon, when Kevin came after me, that it would be such a day. As I was leaving the school with my buddies he came up quickly behind me, put his hand on my shoulder and whipped me around.

"John E.! John E.! What do you think that stands for? John E. Walker! Do you think that's John Edward? No. My dad says it stands for Johnny Walker Black, like the scotch. Your father is nothing but a lousy drunk."

I stood there, stunned. For a second the significance of it didn't register. Then I punched him. I gut-punched him and knocked the breath out of him. He was bigger than I was; we were both surprised. I was scared and didn't know what to do next. If I ran he would certainly catch up to me and beat me up, but I wasn't even thinking of that. I was just standing there with my fists up, ready to punch him again. He looked at me, disgust in his eyes.

"John E. Walker Black," he spat at me, and we watched as he turned on his heel and walked away.

My only mistake was to be on school grounds when I punched him, and within eyeshot of Sister Margaret. She was sitting at her desk correcting papers, having stayed late to 'straighten out' yet another poor schoolboy. When she looked up to ensure that the poor fellow was indeed writing his essay on tardiness and timeliness, she happened to glance out one of the long windows in the old brick building housing our grammar school, St. Joseph's. She saw me punch out that nasty Kevin, and saw him bend over in pain and not hit me back. She tore out of that classroom and down the wide stone stairs moving faster than I thought possible. The long chain of wooden rosary beads hanging from her waist clattered in the wind.

"Johnny," she shouted shrilly, "Johnny, what is going on? Why did you punch Kevin?"

I knew I was doomed. Of all the transgressions in the nuns' rule book, this was one of the worst. I was hoping that my good record of passivism would carry me through and allow me to get only a minor punishment: maybe a week after school, maybe a visit to the principal.

The nuns weren't a bad sort, just usually too busy trying to make everyone study and be responsible. Details were their focus, and heaven forbid you should come under their vigilant gaze. A slip of the tongue, a bit of dirt from a schoolyard scuffle, or an errant shirttail could, if you didn't watch your step, garner you too much negative attention. That's when you might find yourself with after-school detention, writing an essay about the importance of cleanliness. If you forgot and didn't spit your gum out before class, it would wind up on your nose, or if you didn't get your homework done, or whispered in class, you might find yourself sitting under the back table, humiliated. If you got caught flipping baseball cards up against the schoolhouse wall (an enterprise at which I did not excel, and in the pursuit of which I had lost many packs of cards), you would be writing about the evils of gambling. The jokesters, myself included, were often singled out for especially creative punishment, usually of the humiliating sort. If my desk was messy I would be required to empty it out and straighten it up in front of everyone, drawing far too much negative attention to myself. If I opened a pack of Sen-Sen[1] to nibble on and the crackling paper caught Sister Margaret's attention, I would have to bring it to the front of the class to explain to everyone what it was and why I thought it necessary to use it.

My buddies and I thought the nuns got together in the evening and shared their spoils: confiscated gum and candy and chocolate and baseball cards that had disappeared into gigantic pockets hidden in the folds of their long black habits. We imagined that they read aloud our essays about the dangers of gambling or cheating, and laughed over stories of how they frightened this one or humiliated that one.

It was my third-grade teacher, Sister Miriam, who changed my attitude about the nuns. Sure, I still believed there were some nuns who were teaching only out of a bent towards sadistic retribution, but Sister Miriam helped me to see them in a different light. She was pretty and kind, and she smiled at me in a way that made me wonder what she would look like without that stiff wimple. What did nuns do with their hair? Some of the guys said they got it all shaved off or got crew cuts. Did they wear this habit all day long? Did they get up and put it on first thing in the morning, kissing each piece and saying a prayer as they donned it? Why did these women go into the convent in the first place? Why did they embrace such a sterile and monastic life? They didn't seem to have a personal life or even to be women, with their black robes and their long wooden rosaries that clacked as they walked. Once, when I was picking up a baseball at the edge of the schoolyard that bordered the convent, I saw a nun in the praying garden. It had shrubs and stone benches, with statues of saints along the little paths. She walked slowly with her missal, every now and then wiping her eyes with a handkerchief. I wondered what brought her to such a display. The nuns never seemed to have emotions.

Now I stood frozen, fists still clenched, in the shadow of the almighty Sister Margaret. I could see it in her eyes. She wanted only to get back to the convent to some warm chicken soup and fresh

---

[1] Old-fashioned breath freshener. The tiny, stamp-shaped licorice flakes came in small easily-concealed packets.

bread, but this skinny little kid was going to make her stay late. Well, he was going to have to pay.

"Johnny, come into the church. Let's see if the principal can call your mother." Oh geeze. It wasn't just the principal, but my mother too! This was overkill.

The principal was a priest, and he was in the church office. We went into the church, blessed ourselves with holy water that I knew Stanley Morgan had spat into yesterday, and walked down the side aisle that was lit by the massive stained glass windows, our every step echoing loudly in the empty building. We passed the Stations of the Cross, seven through twelve. I always liked the look of Station Eight. The relief was carved from oak and very dramatic. I was trying to focus on these stations, trying to look pious, when Sister Margaret knocked on the big raised-panel oak door at the back of the darkened church.

A deep voice replied, "Come in."

Sister Margaret was all apologies to Father O'Reilly, but he could see right through her.

He too wanted nothing more than to go home, back to the rectory where they were having the leftovers of Mrs. Dennahey's pork roast, which was even better the second night. Father O'Reilly listened to Sister Margaret, and when she was done with her indictment of me, he dismissed her. He stood up, came around the desk, and leaned against it. I stood in front of him like a deer in the headlights of a car.

"Well, Johnny, what do you have to say about all this?"

I figured since I was in so deep already there was no sense in telling the truth now.

"Kevin said that Father Richards was knocking Sister Miriam up, and I was defending her honor." Actually it was rumored Father Richards was becoming too chummy with one of the altar boys, so I felt this was a safe, maybe even welcome, remark.

Father O'Reilly's eyebrows shot up, and he steadied himself on the desk. "What? What did you say?"

I realized that I was in really deep now and had to somehow find a way to swim out.

"Well," I explained, "Kevin was saying these awful things about Father Richards and Sister Miriam." I had never calculated that his next move would be to call Kevin's parents. He believed me and was going to confirm my story. We waited in silence for Kevin and his parents to arrive, Father O'Reilly shuffling through papers while I sat on the large hard oak bench by the door.

Finally Jerome and Lucille Hunt arrived with Kevin in tow, all of them looking flustered and hungry. Father O'Reilly stood in front of Kevin and asked him about the fight. Kevin was obviously scared. All this was because of his remarks to me. He tried to smooth it over.

"What's this all about? Kevin said he didn't do anything," Mr. Hunt started in a menacing tone, but before he could say any more his wife interrupted him. "Buck, calm down and let Father O'Reilly handle this."

Father O'Reilly again asked Kevin what had happened.

"I just told him his old man should get some help because of his drinking."

A blatant lie, but it made me mad. "That's not what you said!"

"Okay, okay. I said he was a drunk, and you were named after his favorite drink." Kevin was in a corner and trying to hold it together. His parents were muttering and nodding in assent. Apparently this was a common topic in the Hunt household.

Father O'Reilly didn't expect this. I had been one of the good kids, never getting into serious trouble, making good grades, working at the mills some evenings. Yet here I was, not only possibly lying, but using malicious, off-color gossip to keep myself from getting into trouble after beating up another kid. I had obviously gone over the edge.

"Kevin, I want you to think very hard about this." Father O'Reilly's tone was grave. "Are you sure this is what you said?" Kevin bobbed his head quickly up and down.

Father O'Reilly said, "Thank you." The look of relief and disbelief on Kevin's face was almost comical. Father O'Reilly apologized to the Hunts for interrupting their dinner and having them come all that way. They left with one backward glance at me, not fully understanding why they were being dismissed and I was staying.

"Well, Johnny, what do you have to say for yourself, now?" This was surely going to be the end of my life. At least that's what I wanted. I wanted God to strike me down right there. I didn't want to face my family, Sister Margaret, Sister Miriam, the kids at school – the whole world would know soon. I would be better off if God just struck me down right here in Father O'Reilly's office. It would be a just punishment. Everyone would feel vindicated, and I wouldn't have to experience the pain and humiliation.

Nothing happened.

God wasn't listening to the silent prayers of an obvious sinner. Father O'Reilly went around to the back of the desk and called my parents.

Chapter 2

John E.'s Family

Before Ma realized the seriousness of Dad's problem, I was named John Edward Walker Black. Years later, on one of her rare visits, she told me what had gone on that day in Father O'Reilly's office. She said that as we walked home from the church in silence she had decided that it was time to make the break. She had to leave him. He wasn't even around to go down to the school with her. He wasn't any help at all in raising me. Steve Black wasn't a bad man, but he was a drunk. He didn't beat her, but he didn't always come home at night, and then she'd find him passed out on the church doorsteps or sleeping it off in what served as our small town's jail. At the mill the next day he would scarcely be able to do his work. She figured it was just a matter of time before he lost his job or was arrested. He would collect his pay on Friday and she wouldn't see him until Sunday night or Monday. There was no family life of any sort, and he usually didn't show her any affection. She was tired of living on the fringes of a good life.

She said that her own mother had worked herself into an early grave, burdened with ten children. Her father had struggled with two jobs to support them. They were kind parents, simple and polite, but Mary never saw them have fun, and she never saw them rest. Finally she had an opportunity to visit an aunt and fun-loving cousin in the city, and she kicked up her heels, visited some clubs, and vowed never to go back to the drudgery of caring for her siblings. She stayed with her aunt for two months, met Steve Black in a club, tried her first martini, lost her virginity, and had me nine months later.

They got married in the city. Then they lied about the marriage date to the folks when they got back home.

Mary was angry and afraid her life would turn out like her mother's. She thought she needed to get out and find happiness before she lost her looks and figure. She'd been working part time as a waitress and cook in the little restaurant down the street. Maybe, she thought, she could start full time down there, but still she wouldn't be able to pay the rent by herself with all the bills she had been struggling to cover. She was weary of trying to make ends meet. She couldn't control her anger when Steve would come home with only part of his paycheck left after a bender.

But then there was that Joe Sweeney, with whom she had had a little fling a couple of years back. He was still sweet on her and had left his wife. She thought she might be able to hook up with him. Joe was fun. He loved to dance and joke and party, but he wouldn't be so much fun with me around. What would people think if she just left her boy? They might understand. She could send me to my other grandparents. They had always liked me, and they were simple, good, honest people. She began to believe that her husband was a bad seed, like his grandfather Whitey, who, after a few too many during lunch one day, had come back to the mill and accidentally killed a guy working on the machinery. The bad seed seemed to skip generations. Harry, Whitey's son, was totally different than his father. Steve and his grandfather Whitey were nothing like me and my grandfather Harry. People would understand her wanting to send me to the farm with Harry and Matilda, where I would get a good upbringing and straighten out. She hoped people would say it was Steve's fault.

My grandparents had a small farm. Harry had worked at the mill like most other people in the town, but he had scrimped and saved his money. When he fell in love with Matilda Worth, whose parents owned the farm a couple miles outside of town, it had been a perfect match. The Worths saw someone who was a hard worker and thrifty, and since they didn't have any kids except Matilda, they brought Harry into the farm and taught him about farming life. He took to it as if he had always been a farm boy. He left the mills behind and found real pleasure on the farm. It was hard work but honest and healthy work. The benefits were good food and fresh air and water, and a quiet life for Harry and Matilda.

They built a little bungalow up on the hill beyond the pasture with a little dirt road running down past the barn to the house. That's where my father was conceived, in that bungalow. It's also where my uncle Charlie, Steve's younger brother, was conceived. Harry and Matilda don't talk much about him. Uncle Charlie was killed in a farm accident before I was born, and they said Steve never got over it. Rumor had it that he was in some way responsible, and that's when he lost his spirit. Steve lost interest in the farm and went to work at the mill. He started going to the city to meet girls and party. Then one night he met Mary, a girl from back home who enjoyed a good time as much as he did. Harry and Matilda were pleased that Steve had found a girl and got married, hoping this would be a leveling factor in his life, and when I came along, they were overjoyed. Steve and Mary took advantage of these good people and left me with them so they could go out dancing. Harry and Matilda kept going on. The farm was their life, and as hard as it was losing Charlie, they kept to their daily routines. I guess that was kind of comforting to them, and with a new grandchild they could almost forget.

So when Ma decided to leave me with them, as selfish as the gesture was, it was the most wonderful thing for Harry and Matilda, and for me it was the beginning of one of the best parts of my life.

Chapter 3

Farm Life

Matilda would be up at five in the morning, fixing coffee and waiting for me to go out with the lantern to gather eggs for breakfast. The chickens were warm and soft, humming quizzically when I would reach under them into the brood boxes for their warm eggs. After the eggs I'd milk Harriet, the old Jersey, so we could have breakfast and so Harry wouldn't have as many cows to milk later on. Harriet was always the heaviest milker so doing her took a good half hour. I got pretty good at it, washing down her udder and stripping the teats at the end. It was a soothing and easy way to wake up, leaning against the warm side of the cow. When I came in with the milk Matilda would set it in a big enamel pan in the kitchen. She would wait for the cream to rise and then skim it off, sometimes saving it for butter, sometimes bottling it to barter with neighbors. The kitchen always smelled a little of sour milk, a smell that I found welcoming. Breakfast would be eggs and sometimes oatmeal or toast, and coffee and milk, lots of milk. On Sundays we'd have bacon or sausages.

Matilda had what she called a kitchen garden, but really it was a very big garden. She'd grow most of what we needed and then some. She'd can what we couldn't eat right away and then she'd barter or give the rest away. People were always stopping in to trade for eggs or milk or vegetables, to have a glass of milk or cup of tea, and to share the town gossip. We'd get all manner of things in return: sometimes a side of bacon, a ham, or a live duck or goose. One afternoon someone brought by a goat. It was the most cunning animal I had ever seen. It could open almost any gate and run off, but once the sky was dark that goat was waiting by the barn, wanting to get back in.

Harry grew corn for the cows, and hay too. The autumn was a busy time with bringing in the second hay, and a neighboring farmer would come and help do the corn. We'd put it up in the old silo where it would store pretty well and keep the cows in feed until spring.

Harry kept bees too, and I was fascinated with them. Every spring he would don his white suit and gloves and a veiled hat, and stoke up the smoker with burlap that he lit and got to smoking. He'd blow the smoke into the entrance of the hive a couple of times, and some of what he called the "guard bees" would start buzzing around and pestering him. After five or ten minutes he'd pry off the top of the hive and blow some more smoke down in there. I stood at a distance, hearing the level of humming rise every time he blew the smoke in or when he removed a super[2] to check for the queen or to see if the bees were filling up the combs the way they should be.

In late spring and late summer he would take honey out. He said the late spring was good after a big honey flow, and the late summer would still allow the bees to stock up with goldenrod and Joe Pye weed in time for winter. I could see that he loved the bees and tried to be careful of every one of his "girls." He'd talk in soothing tones to them and tell them not to worry. Sometimes he'd take me out when one of the neighbors came by with news of a swarm. He'd keep a small empty hive set up and ready to go for these occasions. He'd get his bee stuff together and we'd jump into the old pickup in the evening, and off we'd go. When we got there we would suit up. If the swarm was in a bush or low branch close enough to the ground, he would put a sheet on the ground under them. Then he'd put the hive on top of the sheet and take the top cover off. He'd start the smoker and then just shake the branch they were hanging from. The bees were like a big loose cluster of grapes, and when he shook the branch they fell like globs of water onto the

---

[2] A section of a beehive comprised of a stackable topless and bottomless wooden box with frames "hanging" inside for honey comb.

open hive. A few of them flew up and buzzed around, but if he shook the branch carefully and with enough vigor the first time, they would start to go into the frames of the hive. They were, after all, looking for a home, he told me. They were happy to have a clean dry spot to start a new family. Gradually, once the queen made her way in, every other bee slowly followed. By dark all the bees were in except for a few mortalities.

Harry would put the top cover on and put a board over the front opening. He would tape it all down so it would all stay together, and we would put it in the back of the truck. The next morning he'd remove the board, and we'd check them out. He'd put a sugar water feeding jar in their entrance, and pretty soon they would be coming and going like an old established hive. He'd keep the new hive ten to twelve feet from the other hives so there wouldn't be too much looting, and he liked to face the entrance east so that the early morning sun warmed them and got them started early on their rounds through the flowers in the neighborhood. I loved the bees and loved doing bee work with him.

Harry was a tall lanky man. "Sinewy," folks said. I liked the way he sauntered down the dusty driveway from the barn with the pails in his hand. It was a solid look, an honest gait. Matilda was short and somewhat stocky. Her breasts had drooped from carrying children, but they still puffed out the broad apron.

Harry and Matilda had kept the old wood-burning cook stove in their kitchen, while the townspeople were going to gas and some to electric. I was expected to split the larger wood down to a manageable size for the stove, which was a warm and handsome piece. Matilda used the smaller pieces of wood to keep it at just the right temperature for special baking, like breads and pies. A big kettle of water was always sitting on it. Even though they had a kitchen sink and running indoor water Harry and Matilda preferred the well water and I would be sent out to pump the water up and bring it in. Things were somewhat old-fashioned on the farm. They even still had an outhouse, which always intrigued me as a child but held less allure as I aged. It wasn't the smell that bothered me; it was the spiders.

For kids a farm is a fascinating place. They see the full cycle of life: baby animals, adult animals, animals breeding and birthing, chickens laying the eggs, and crops sown, grown, and reaped. Kids learn some pretty harsh lessons on a farm. They can lose their pets to nature and to the dinner table, and without a good loving family to provide a balance, a child could become hardened.

I thrived out on the farm, and it didn't even bother me when the kids called me a hick because I knew many of them were jealous. When given the opportunity to visit they jumped at it. Harry and Matilda taught me all the important things about life: how essential honesty is, and fairness, and kindness, and hard work, and love.

Matilda always said, "God loves you, and don't let any person tell you otherwise, because if someone tells you otherwise, they don't know anything about God. I could never understand why all these church people insisted on making us feel bad about ourselves. God wouldn't condone that; God loves us. What is that all about? What was this original sin all about? What is it about babies being born with any kinda sin? Babies aren't born with sin – that's hokum. Where did that come from? Those religious folk were always trying to make you feel bad about something. I don't think the other religions were that much better than the Catholics, either. The Baptists were all hellfire and brimstone. Little Susie Card, she was always coming in talking about how they 'gotta drive the devil out of her.' They just wanted us to buy our way into heaven, tithing them if they kept us feeling guilty about something. And what was that about God not accepting that we had feelings for people until we got married? After marriage it was okay to have those unclean thoughts about them? But before, it wasn't okay? God doesn't think like that. God understands that love is love. Well, I gotta say, they've got pretty good schools though. Strict, with education. It's that other stuff that drives me to the bughouse."

Matilda was full of these insights about life and often spouted her philosophical theories while she was cooking or cleaning or while we were out hoeing the kitchen garden. Harry and I listened and mostly thought it was all good sense, until she got on a high and mighty tangent about pol-o-tics. She thought many politicians were crooks and scoundrels. Once she got on this subject she held onto it and shook it like a bull terrier.

Harry and Matilda had a common sense that I understood and admired, but I had no idea that it sometimes put them at odds with some of the townsfolk.

Chapter 4

Work at the Mill

While I was still young, barely out of grade school, I started work at the mill. My first position at the mill was as a doffer. I would remove the bobbins of full thread and replace them with empty ones, and then set up the threads on each bobbin so that when the machine started to spin the thread onto the bobbin, that thread wouldn't come loose and the bobbin would fill up. I'd put the full bobbins into a crate and pile the crates up at the end of the machine rows, and the bigger guys would come along with a cart and pick them all up. This was a fairly safe job and could be done without much supervision. The floor supervisors liked me because I was quick and didn't dawdle like some of the other doffers. I kept up with the winders on the second floor, and there wasn't a pile up of empty cartons.

I worked after school and during the summer except for Sundays for twelve cents a hour. I would set up a row of twenty bobbins on the machine and gradually I was able to do five winding machines, one after the other. It kept me running. I would pick the end of the thread from where it was fed out from the winding machine and hook it onto the tab on the bobbin. I would do this twenty times per machine. The winder would follow me and start the machines up. When he threw the switch on the machine the thread would start spinning around and around that bobbin. The arm would move the thread up and down, winding it so there was an even distribution on the spool. When it was full the winder would turn it off. I would cut the thread, pull the bobbin off, put it into the carton, and put an empty one on and start over again. Younger people were preferred for this job because we were short, down closer to where the bobbins were, and our fingers were more nimble. We could move along pretty quickly cutting and pulling the bobbins off. My winder liked me because I was fast and because the more bobbins he could do the more money he made. When we first started out they put us on coat thread because it was heavier and not so liable to break. As we gained experience they would move us up to finer sewing threads. Our small fingers allowed us to thread through the eye that distributed the thread. If a thread broke the winder would stop the machine and I'd be there to try to make a smooth splice to the broken ends. Then he'd start the machine up again.

On weekdays when I got out of school I would go down to the mill and work until 6, run home to eat dinner, and then do my homework if I didn't fall asleep first. Harry and Matilda took up the slack with the evening chores because they saw how this work was a balance to my farm work. But I was still required to get most of my morning chores done.

When the mill was humming the clatter was so loud I could barely hear people shout to me. The air always had a thin haze of cotton dust hanging in it that would settle onto the machines and window sills and floor after we knocked off in the evening. The place got swept daily and sometimes hourly, depending on the threads. I would get an extra ten cents a day if I was able to both sweep and get my doffing job done. They had to be careful about the cotton dust because if it got too thick it could ignite. It did once in a Vermont textile mill and a whole wing of the mill blew up. Two people were killed when the roof beams collapsed. They were lucky it was at the end of the shift or there could have been more. Some of the old timers got "grey lung" from the cotton dust and coughed their way into the morgue.

The winding room was on the second floor. The dyeing room was on the first floor, so you could look out the window and see the river running yellow or red or blue, or whatever color the cotton was being dyed that day. That was a part of the river that was diverted into the canal under the mill and it was also what drove the turbines to power the machinery with big gears and gigantic leather belts. The stairs between the floors were big, wide, and solid wood. When the shift let out the march of workers down those stairs was one of my favorite sounds. The wooden floors were dark with the oil that kept the machinery running smoothly. The oil men tended the big mechanical monsters with dedication, always able to find a nut to fit a bolt or a fitting that had sheared off. I loved to visit them in their little closet and look into the hundreds of bins of screws and nuts and bolts and miscellaneous parts, finding treasures like magnifying lenses that they would let me pop into my pocket to show to my buddies at school the next day or give to the younger kids, who would burn up leaves and fry ants. Even on the sunniest days the skylights in the third-floor roof gave a grey light that filtered down through the cotton dust, giving the eerie appearance that God Himself was supervising that day.

The mill workers were a varied lot. Some became dulled by the unrelenting monotony of the job. Eventually they were not even motivated enough to move up into another position, and so they stayed, spending years at the same machine doing the same mind-numbing work. Others were interested in the processes they saw around them. They would work up from the winding room to become supervisors or shop stewards. Many of these people were immigrants from Canada or Ireland or Sweden, and they knew the value of a dollar and hard work. Some were swamp Yankees who were shrewd and watchful and swollen with entitlement. The one thing they had in common was the mill, and most of them lived within a stone's throw of it.

Chapter 5

The Town, the River and the Lake

Most workers lived in town, close to the mill, where rows of sturdy two-family houses ran one upon the other. They were all painted white and had picket fences, and old maple and elm trees lined the streets, sheltering the homes with their shade. Each two-storey duplex was big enough for two families of six, and close enough to the mill for people to walk to work by crossing the footbridge. Every morning the road and sidewalk were full of workers with lunch pails heading down to the mill, and every evening the road was choked with them returning home for dinner. The whole town smelled of cabbage and corned beef, or sauerkraut and bratwurst, or chicken and biscuits, and always of bread. Behind the houses large clotheslines separated the yards.

There was a big ballpark with a grandstand where the men's baseball clubs played serious baseball. Weekends brought ballgames and picnics and dances and concerts. There was a school built by the mill. The mill also had a company store on Main Street that sold everything from soap to coal. The mill was fair and generous and good to the people. For that they got good work and people who returned year after year and sent their children to work there. Turnover was low and a dependable workforce was always close by.

Nestled between two rows of hills, the town was beautiful. The river, flowing northwest to southeast, funneled down between the hills and was dammed to create a lake that backed up more than a mile and gave the mill a ready source of power. The section of it that had been diverted to a canal through the mill served also as the dumping trough for the washing and dyeing water. The little valley had enough flat land to accommodate the mill, houses, churches, school, and small downtown. The downtown, although modest, met the townspeople's basic needs with a butcher, a grocer, a baker, several dry goods stores, a pharmacy with a soda fountain, and a boarding-house. For entertainment they had a library, a couple of bars, a diner with booths, a men's club, and the beautiful lake where people boated and swam. On the outskirts a pool hall served food and had room enough to dance. On the corner near the main thoroughfare was a package store. Three churches and a convent supported a parochial school, orphanage and old-age home. Rounding out the basic requirements for this small town were a funeral parlor, volunteer fire department, and small police force.

Visitors driving over the hill and descending into the valley where the mill town nestled might think they were coming into an idyllic world, a picture-perfect little village with its church steeples, mill tower, and smoke drifting from the chimneys. It called to them, making them yearn for this seemingly simple life.

Behind the beautiful façade it did not differ much from other towns. It had a harder side of life where men went home to good wives and good dinners and beat them if dinner wasn't just to their liking, where men drank themselves into a stupor night after night and where some mothers beat their children and some fathers molested them. The bars were busy after work, and often wives went down at the barkeep's behest to bring their husbands home before closing. Always there were good people who were the backbone of the town, who kept it safe; and then there were the others, small in numbers but who could make life difficult for everyone.

I grew up in the town, I appreciated the mill, and I loved my grandparents at the farm. I felt I had the best life in the world. Even school was enticing, as it brought the outside world, which often felt so far away, within my grasp. In so many ways it showed not only another side of life, but also how very much our little world had in common with the world outside it.

Seasons kept life churning in the village, and when spring came everyone was ready for the change. The sterility of winter gave way to gentle green sprouts. People were optimistic and giddy with the heady smells of flowers and earth. Bees were holding court in the apple orchard and birds were in the mulberries. The community gardens were plowed and those folks who still had outhouses dug new pits and moved them. Even with all the mud, we loved it. Early evenings in the shadow of the surrounding hills were warm and promising, and the peepers, first one or two at a time, but finally the whole population peeped so wildly they sounded like a thousand sleigh bells. Matilda would say that whatever you were doing that first evening you heard the peepers was what you would be doing the rest of the year. We loved walking down the sidewalks past homes with their lights pouring into the street from windows long closed and now open.

A springtime farm would be full of bouncing babies. Little goats, unsteady on their feet for a day or two, were soon springing around like kids. A brood chicken, finally allowed a clutch of eggs, walked purposefully about with her new flock, pulling blades of grass. Her little fuzz-ball chicks scurried to keep up and tried pulling on the grass as though they were old pros. Calves finding their legs and their mothers' teats looked like awkward kids just trying out their new stilts, stiff and spread-legged like a sawhorse.

The spring river would bring incredible water flow. Below the dam by the big flats the ice sheets melted and were driven down the stream by heavy rain and runoff, wearing away the bark of the trees closest to the shore. I could see the toll of the heavy ice crashing against them; they were old, hardened, and deformed by the spring melts. These trees had survived and had even become part of the river, their roots bared, holding onto the rocks and riverbank, branches almost touching the water. One sometimes succumbed to the erosion by gently falling in, but even then it would continue to grow and leaf out and protect the denizens of the river below, roots in the shore, branches in the water. Spring water was not as dangerous as winter ice. Its perils were obvious, and where the water dropped crashing from ledge to ledge through the ravines, its roar could be heard long before it was seen.

I was busy going from the farm to the school to the mill. Occasionally I would get a Saturday off from the mill, and Grandpa Harry would teach me how to fish. We had a favorite spot, on the south side of the lake just above the dam. A dirt path following the lake was lined with boulders and trees worn smooth from a regular flow of fishermen. Harry said they were a sloppy lot; sometimes a coffee can was left by the bank, worms gone, or a beer bottle discarded, or someone would forget an empty tobacco tin. I loved exploring the shore, the source of all manner of wildlife: frogs and snakes, muskrat, goose, heron, deer, wildflowers and berries. All of it was wonderful and exciting.

In summer these paths along the shore had an allure all their own. When people in town were hot and fanning themselves the folks down by the lake shores would be cool. The north side had a beach where moored boats competed with swimmers and the south side at the bottom of a steep hill was mossy and dark. Here and there a stone outcropping was wide and flat enough to lounge around on. Lying on one of these rock ledges with a towel tucked under my head I would easily fall asleep, mesmerized by the gentle breeze and distant hiss of the water falling over the dam. In the summer the best fishing was in the early morning and again around sundown, when the fish were prowling for a meal. Sometimes in the river below the dam you would see the dark shadowy figure of a trophy trout slowly swimming along the edges of the pool, searching for the one misjudgment of a minnow or frog that would become dinner.

In autumn, leaves swirled down through the water, settling at the bottom of pools or washing down to the dam to pile up and be raked away. Crawfish would be scurrying to find the last bits of insects, and frogs looked for good hibernating spots.

The autumn farm was buzzing with activity with everyone making an effort to get the harvest picked and stored before the cold put an end to it. Autumn also meant the exciting town agricultural fair with animal tents of chickens, sheep, goats and pigs. First prize for the oxen pulls always went to old Sparkie Nelson, who was anything but sparky. Slight and quiet, he would drive his team with sweet and gentle words and whistles and never flick his little whip.

But the team dove into the ground and pulled with a force that always took home the prize, to the amazement and envy of the bulky men who hollered and snapped at the oxen, whose eyes showed their whites as they craned to look at their loud and fearsome drivers. A long line formed at the Ferris wheel out beyond the pig tent. Girls were grooming their sheep, and women proudly displayed their blue-ribbon apple pies. Farmers in overalls propped up gigantic cornstalks that scraped the top of the tent. Kids got silly on cotton candy. Men stood around the booth with the spinning wheel hoping to win a pack of cigarettes for their five-cent bet, the wheel at first sounding like the drone of an insect but then slowing down to clack at each nail until the number was called. Teens tried to get the Ferris wheel to stop at the top so they could kiss their girlfriends. Boys popped balloons with darts to win a teddy bear. Autumn fairs brought all the excitement of the harvest to a close.

In autumn and winter the school would hold dances for us. We would all be excited and anxious to arrive but uncomfortable and nervous once we did. In the chairs lined up along both sides of the gymnasium mostly girls sat on one side and mostly boys on the other. In a separate area boys would hang around the ping pong table or the chessboards. Some of the older boys would be out near the dance floor, where all the girls were dancing with one another and stealing glances at the ping pong area, whispering among themselves and giggling. I never understood all the giggling. I didn't know whether being the object of it would be a good thing or more embarrassing. But it was not a concern for me as I stood shyly near the corner with a couple of other boys, more comfortable being an observer.

In winter we would go sliding down the hillside roads. From uphill where the bosses lived to the bottom where the workers were, we would *fly* down these hills, refining the course as we went. A little more snow packed and banked up here, a little less there, and we had a course we could steer down from top to bottom. Men would set up ice-fishing jigs on the lake and wait for the flags to fly up to signal a bite. We would skate on the frozen ice and have big bonfires there at night. The older boys would find a bottle to pass around, and the girls would giggle and fall off the benches. Jessy Handley once ran his sled into a milk pail that was frozen solid into the ground, and Luigi the barber sewed up the cut over his eyebrow.

The winter river behind the big flats hid the teeming life below. Layer upon layer of ice built up thickly each time a rivulet or stray drop hit the frigid air, and fantastic sculptures of blue ice formed on the boulders. In many places the water rushed underneath, visible only through little windows. This was a dangerous time for those believing it safe to cross the river. Moving water would make the bizarrely formed icecap as thick as a tree in some areas and thin as paper in others. Woe to the unknowing soul who didn't pick the safe crossing.

We took the river for granted, but it was our life. It fed us on its incessant flow to the sea. It was where we worked and where we played. It watered our homes and gardens and washed away our grime. It was our constant companion, that distant roar of the rushing flow, or trickle of the little rivulets, or the stillness of the lake. No one would have said it was why our little town grew up on its shores or even have given it another thought. But this mighty Shetucket River was as important to us as the sun and the air.

Chapter 6

Fishing With Gerry

It was spring, and Gerry Murphy and I headed off to the river for some serious fishing. We walked down the worn path that ran alongside the lake above the dam. Little puffs of dust followed our steps. We had two Coca-Colas and two bologna sandwiches Uncle Jake had made in the butcher shop, slathered in mustard and wrapped in butcher paper with a half pickle in the folds. I had the old pole Grandpa Harry had given me, with its chipped cork handle and missing a loop. I loved it and thought it had probably been my dad's. Gerry had an old pole too, passed down from brother to brother to him. He would probably have to pass it on to his younger brothers.

It was Sunday and felt like the most wonderful day of the year. I had nothing to do but go fishing. Harry said he could manage what was going on around the farm, and it was a day off from the mill. The sky was a bright blue, and the air was warming up. I thought it wouldn't be early enough to catch any whoppers but I didn't care. We could just sit there and watch the world go by. We spread ourselves out on the ledge that protruded beyond the rest, hiding a cove on one side and overlooking the lake on the other. Gerry put our Cokes in the water while I put a struggling worm on the hook and tossed my line as far across the pool as it would reach without getting tangled. Almost immediately I got a hit. BAM! The fish hit hard and started off in the other direction. I pulled back hard against it to set the hook, and started to reel it towards me. It swam this way and that, in the opposite direction, but always losing ground to the inevitable sway of the reel. I saw a flash of dark fish. It looked like a decent-sized bass. I got it up close to the ledge and was able to get it off the hook without losing it. I cut a small branch from an overhanging maple, stripped off all the leaves and small branches except the bottom branch, and threaded the growing end up through the fish's gill and out its mouth. This was a fish to bring home and have for dinner! I was hoping for one more so it would be a good meal for us all. The second or third cast might bring another fish, but it was usually the first that brought the bite, and after that the area cooled off, others becoming more wary. Gerry cast after I landed my bass, but no bite followed.

    We settled down to watch the rowboats and canoes move slowly up and down the lake. We talked about the mill, opening our sandwiches and laughing between bites about the German guy whose wife came to escort him home to try to make sure he wouldn't be stopping down at the bar; her apron would be flying and she'd be sputtering German at him all the way. As we were eating we heard laughing and talking on the path above. It sounded like a man and a woman. I knew there was a fishing camp further down the path but I had rarely seen people go down there, and never a woman.

    I scrambled up the bank and tried to peek through the bushes without being seen. Gerry climbed up next to me. I could see the two stumbling down the path, the man's arm around the woman's shoulder and the woman's arm around his waist. They were animated, talking and then bending over laughing, and I could see a beer bottle in the man's hand. He paused to take a swig, and they continued on. I thought I recognized the guy from the mill, but I didn't recognize the woman. Gerry and I lowered ourselves back down to the ledge and discussed what we had seen. Gerry said his oldest brother had been spending time down at the fishing camp, and when his father found out he beat the tar out of him. Gerry and his brothers couldn't understand the trouble with spending time fishing. We looked at each other and instantaneously hatched a plan to find out more about the fishing camp. In minutes we had reeled in our lines, thrown the soggy worms from the hooks back into the river, and stashed the poles up under some bushes along with our lunch papers and my bass, now quite dead.

Down the path we ran until we figured we were within hearing distance of the couple, who could possibly be around the next bend. Then we sneaked along, hoping to hear them before they heard us. As we rounded the bend we ran headlong into two big guys coming from the opposite direction. I ran my face right into Buck Hunt's big hard beer belly. It knocked me over. They looked at us, as surprised as we were, but as I gasped in shock, Buck's demeanor changed to rage. I picked myself up, wheeled around, and flew off in the direction we had just come from, Gerry pounding the ground behind me. I could hear Buck cussing at us and charging along. He was quicker than I expected, but gradually the sound of him and the other guy receded, and we ducked into some bushes, panting. We tried to quiet ourselves, and in a minute they passed us, laughing and joking about the damned nosey brats and what they would have done if they had gotten ahold of us. Once we were sure they were gone we backtracked to where our poles were and headed home. The excitement had totally taken away the allure of fishing, and my fish had disappeared. Some furred or feathered opportunist had gotten the better of that deal.

Chapter 7

The Fishing Camp

The adventure at the river was a topic of conversation for Gerry and me for weeks to come. What happened to the couple? Where did Buck Hunt and his buddy come from? If the guy was fishing, what was he doing without his pole? We started to make up fantastic stories, but none of them beat the truth when we finally found it out.

Summer was at its peak, beautiful, hot, and green. The farm was a great place during the summer. When we had to do the haying some of my buddies would come over and we would help Harry. We'd run behind the baler, throwing the bales onto the flatbed trailer, while someone up on top of the trailer stacked them high as a house, climbing the pile like a mountain to put the next one on. Matilda would make us big fried chicken lunches and a thermos of swizzle[3] to slake our thirst.

We'd watch the havoc that haying brought to the animal community. Sitting there eating lunch, we'd see a fox come cautiously out to the edge of the new-mown field and grab disoriented mice whose homes had been destroyed. Little baby rabbits would hop about dazed, looking for what had once been their burrow entrance. Snakes moved through quickly before a hawk sighted them. Haying made us hungry and thirsty and itchy, and

---

[3] Also called switchel.—A traditional drink originating in the Caribbean and served to thirsty farmers during hay harvest time. It was usually made by adding molasses, honey or maple syrup to water and mixing in ginger and vinegar.

when we were done we were always allowed to head down to the lake for a swim before collapsing into our beds.

Late that afternoon, after all the hay was up, we headed down to the lake on the path towards the fisherman's camp. We stripped down to our skivvies, Gerry and Larry and Buddy and I. We used the rope swing to sway way out over the deepest part of the pool before letting go and plopping down with a splash. If we misjudged the drop we might end up with a scraped leg or shoulder from hitting the rocks on the edges. The ruckus scattered the fish so much they swam away in big swirls. We were having a fine time rinsing the sweat and grass off, throwing in rocks and diving after them, or throwing a larger rock and holding on without letting go so we'd be pulled down to the bottom without any effort. Then we'd let go when we hit bottom. Small fish were nipping at our toes, making us splash and scream. We told fantastic stories to each other about snapping turtles biting off toes or pulling small kids down to their dens. Of course we had never heard any of this as gospel truth, and turtles don't have dens, but it was good for scary story stuff. Larry grabbed Buddy's foot and pulled him down, and he screamed. We loved it. If one of us jumped too close to the shore, instead of climbing back up the rock ledge we waded into shore, and if not careful cut our feet on the freshwater clams. As we were getting ready to leave Gerry and I decided to share our secret story of the last time we were down at the fishing hole. As we told Larry and Buddy, the tale grew even more fantastic and mysterious. We could see their excitement building. Should we all sneak down to the camp and see what it looked like? See if anybody was there? Check it out?

We struggled madly to get the clothes onto our still-damp bodies. We scrambled up the bank and made off towards the camp, walking quietly and whispering as we went, in case we met someone around the next bend. The dirt path roughly paralleled the river, with bushes and flowers and trees alongside. Because it lay north of the steep hill, it was cool in the summer heat. The shore on the other side was still sunlit at this time of day. It was early evening and the sun shone down between the hills that cradled the lake, sometimes glistening off the water.

We heard a splash, then voices. Hushing each other we moved along slowly, hiding in the bushes bordering the lake. There in the secluded cove was a naked man. A woman on the bank threw him a bar of soap that he used to lather up his armpits, his face, his privates, his hair. He scrubbed and scrubbed, with the woman's enthusiastic encouragement. We heard her say something about being clean as a whistle. He cajoled her, inviting her in, but she responded that she didn't have all day. Once he realized that she wasn't to be persuaded he got out and dried off. He got his pants and shoes on, and as she was retrieving the bar of soap and putting it into the can she picked up from the bank, he grabbed her around the waist from behind. He groped for her breasts and started kissing her hair and neck. He pressed himself against her. She protested some but then giggled and pushed back against him. He didn't even take his pants off, but unzipped his fly and pulled up her dress from behind. He pushed into her with a groan as she grunted and steadied herself against the bank. After a few quick thrusts he arched his back and groaned again. We all stood there in wide-eyed awe, not even breathing. From the farm I had a basic understanding of animal husbandry, and I had seen dogs in town going at it, but I had never before seen two people doing it. I was struck by the thought that it did not seem so much different. We all exhaled slowly together.

"Wow," Gerry said under his breath.

We waited as they straightened up their clothes and disappeared on a steep path up the wooded hill. We sat there quietly, thinking about what we had just seen.

"I've seen my sister and her boyfriend necking before, but I've never seen anything like that." Buddy's tone was hushed.

None of us was old enough or experienced enough to act nonchalant about it. Under most circumstances we would have been pushing each other back and forth in embarrassment, but a corner had been turned here. On some level each of us knew that this was an important moment, one that showed us a flash of our futures, of our parents, of all couples, of all human beings. It was such a simple and honest act of pleasure and love. It was obvious that they both enjoyed it, and that they cared for one another.

We started to get up to leave when we heard someone else coming down the path. Two guys were whistling and jiggling silver dollars in their pockets, both with their hair combed, each carrying a paper bag. They came so close we could smell the cologne on them. I recognized one as a mill worker who usually wore coveralls and worked on the machinery. He whistled while he worked too. We began to realize just what kind of a fishing camp this was.

Chapter 8

Bullhead Fishing

It would be several weeks before we could get to the lake again, and you can bet that was the place we most wanted to be. Fishing and swimming were diminished by the overpowering desire to get down to the camp road again. Even bullhead fishing with Grandpa Harry didn't hold the allure it once did, when we used to head out at sunset for the lake up at the top of the hill. It wasn't a big lake, and it wasn't very deep, but in it were some of the most lovely bullheads. We would settle in at the end of the small dock at dusk, with Harry lighting the kerosene lantern so we could see to bait our hooks and take the fish off them. Worms didn't have to be too fresh for bullheads. Sometimes I thought, the stinkier the better, but I myself couldn't stand worms too close to dead. We'd bait, and cast out a little way, letting the line settle down to the bottom because bullheads are bottom-feeders. It was never long before one or the other of us got a bite, and what a battle it would be. These fish are fierce fighters. Even in the summer we could usually catch some, although the best fishing would start at apple-blossom time. This was when they were spawning, and they would almost jump out of the water onto the dock. It was a big deal to catch the first fish, and Harry always acted pleased when it was me.

"Geeze-us, that's a whopper. Watch out he doesn't break the line."

He'd reel his line in and wait until I landed the fish before he'd cast again. I figured it was half out of courtesy and half out of pride and sheer joy in his grandson's good luck. Harry showed me how to hold my catch so I wouldn't get stuck by its sharp fins: grabbing it from underneath by slipping my hand up its belly as it hung from the line, putting my first two fingers over the fins and the rest of my hand around the belly. The fins usually stayed rigid enough for me to grab tight and get the hook out, but sometimes it would move its fins and make a strange grunting sound. I had to be careful getting the hook out too; these guys could bite and didn't want to let go once they did.

Bullheads were like prehistoric creatures. When Harry was back home, cleaning them on a newspaper on the kitchen table, he would cut off the heads and then skin the body. They were still alive. He showed me how the dismembered head would grab at a pencil put in its mouth. I was fascinated. Even in the morning some heads were still able to snap at things, and it would get us all to laughing to watch the cats when we put these unbelievable heads outside for them. I had a soft spot for bullheads; they were so primal. I wanted them to live as much as they wanted to, and I disliked having one of them swallow the hook. Harry had a number of tricks to get it out, none of them pleasant. Hooks were not something to be squandered, however, and he would retrieve them. I think he knew that it wasn't squeamishness that kept me from pulling the hook out, but just a desire to see these creatures survive. I didn't mind it for trout. Trout died within minutes of taking them out of the water, and I had no bad feelings about cleaning a dead fish. I got pretty good at sensing the instant a fish was on the line and setting the hook in its jaw. This way I wouldn't have to go through the unpleasant experience of ripping a hook from its stomach.

We went fishing this evening, and the bullheads weren't biting much. Harry lit the lantern, and the familiar smell of kerosene brought a comforting sense of tradition. We baited our hooks and cast out about twenty-five feet. It was dusk, and immediately a bass hit Harry's worm before it could even sink, flashing out of the water – a surprising event, this evening bass bite.

Harry pulled back hard with his pole, bending it over, trying to sink the hook. As he pulled the fish jumped out of the water again, flapped back and forth once, and spit the hook out. Harry cursed and reeled the line back in. He re-baited his hook and cast his line again, while I waited in patient expectation for a bite. I started to talk about trout fishing down by the lake, then about seeing people go down to the fisherman's camp. My mind kept drifting back to the lake and to that particular afternoon when we had gone swimming. I thought this was innocent enough talk. Harry surprised me with his response.

"You know that's not a fishermen's camp."

I couldn't tell if this was a question or a statement.

"What?" I asked, surprised at his straightforwardness and his willingness to touch on this subject.

"You know that's not a fishermen's camp." It was a statement.

"Yeah," I said, figuring that if I seemed knowledgeable about it he might continue. I wanted to know more.

"That's been there for years, before you were born. We used to call it Jenny's Way, because Jenny started it."

I was quiet, waiting for more, barely breathing.

Harry went on, "I went to school with Jenny. She was a real beauty. She married young, to a man everyone called Lucky, Lucky O'Sullivan. She barely got out of high school before she was married and pregnant. Lucky was a football player and a star athlete in high school, earning his letter and a possible scholarship to a local college. When Jenny got pregnant so soon he did the right thing, he married her. But it spoiled Lucky's chance to go to college, and he got mean. He got a job stocking at the market, a dead end job, he thought. Lucky was never willing to work hard and look past the present to the possibility of moving up. He was too busy thinking about his lost opportunity. Reality is, he probably wouldn't have done well in college. He wasn't that smart, and he wasn't that good an athlete either. He started drinking, and pretty soon he was knocking Jenny around. We wouldn't see her around for a week, and then when someone would run into her she'd have the yellow and purple of old bruise marks on her face or arms. She almost lost her baby, and one morning when she couldn't take it anymore, after Lucky went to work she ran away.

"No one would take her in. Her mother didn't have much and she didn't like Lucky, and she sure didn't want her pregnant daughter back. Jenny stayed at a girlfriend's that first night, but the family asked her politely to leave. She was afraid to go back to Lucky, afraid he would certainly make her lose the baby, if not kill her outright.

"The next day, after walking around the town trying to figure out what to do, she wandered up to a fisherman's cottage on the hill above the lake, in that beautiful ravine. She had very little money, and she didn't have a job, but her girlfriends from school would bring food up to her. When the baby came they helped her then too. I heard that Alice, the old lady who lives over the butcher shop, went up to help her give birth.

"Jenny had a baby as beautiful as she was, and she named her Lily. She tried to stay up there and look for work too. Some of the people in town knew what had been going on, but Lucky had been a sort of hometown hero and they felt it was all Jenny's own doing. She couldn't get anyone to take care of the baby, couldn't work, and couldn't get a cheap rent. Sometimes one of her old boyfriends from school would take her down to the tavern for dinner, and she'd have the baby in the booth with her. He'd escort her back to the cottage and, well, one thing led to another until she had a regular business up there, not just her old beau but a few others too. Do you know what I'm saying?" I nodded gravely. "So that's how it got to be called Jenny's Way."

"Wow, Harry, have you ever been up there?" It seemed like an innocent question when I first said it.

"Yeah, I used to go up there too, but not often, and I was careful not to be seen. On Friday nights, after I got my pay envelope, I would wander the streets of town looking for something to do. Then pretty soon my feet would turn towards that path by the dam that led upriver along the lake. I loved her. I think pretty much all the guys did. She was sweet and pretty, and she had been wronged by the man she loved. We saw her as a victim, and we wanted to help and protect her, and we did. Anyone who visited brought her food, and then they brought her other things, too: a blanket, or a towel, or kerosene, or toilet paper. She was able to make out okay. The boys didn't always want 'favors.' Sometimes they just wanted to hang around, play games, drink and gab, but they still brought some beer, or hot dogs.

"Jenny tried to have friends visit at night when Lily was sleeping, but sometimes Lily was watched by a younger girl, Sally, who was a pal of Jenny's. Well, it wasn't long before Sally was part of the business too. The funny thing is, no one really saw this as bad or as a business. Jenny and Sally were clean and decent people who had just had some hard knocks in life. Most townspeople just left them alone. Some years later Sally married one of her clients from a nearby town. She had a family and settled down."

"Is Jenny still there?"

"Yes, I hear she's taking care of Rachael, her granddaughter."

I jumped and looked at Harry. "Rachael? Rachael O'Sullivan?"

I went to school with Rachael. She was quiet and sweet, and most of the boys had a crush on her. Now I understood how Jenny could do it. A person like Rachael had lots of boys who would want to help her. If her grandmother were anything like her, well, I'd want to help her out too.

After that first bullhead hit the fish weren't biting at all, and I didn't care one bit. Harry reeled his line in, then pulled the worm off and threw it in the water, a sure signal that fishing was over.

"I just happened to hear that you were seen up that way, up on Jenny's Way," he said, "and I wanted you to know the whole story."

I wondered how he'd heard I'd been up that way, spying on the path and its travelers.

Chapter 9

Uncle Jake

Harry wasn't much of a talker, but this night he had outdone himself. I wanted to know more; I doubted that was the whole story. I had all sorts of questions, but I knew that he didn't have more to say then, and badgering him was not the method to get more from him.

Walking home we passed through the edge of town. I could see lights on in the houses. I always liked looking into people's houses as I walked by in the evening. They looked warm and cozy. They pulled me in, and it gave me a feeling of well-being to see fathers sitting in their armchairs reading the papers, in the warm glow of a floor lamp, and mothers in their armchairs knitting or crocheting. Once in a while I'd smell a home-cooked meal getting warmed up for a late-comer. Lights were going out in the upstairs windows as the kids went to bed. The evening was winding down, calmly, quietly. If we were later than usual, a drunken man would be stumbling home. Sometimes a man sitting on his stoop in the dusk would light up a cigarette, the end glowing brighter as he inhaled, and I could hear him sigh out the smoke.

As we passed Uncle Jake's butcher shop I could see that the side door was open and light was pouring out into the alley. A truck was backed up there and two guys were standing near the door, looking nervous. I could hear Uncle Jake swearing.

"What the hell were you thinking? This isn't the time of year to take deer. They're no good now, full of worms, and you don't know if you're taking a doe with a yearling or what you've got, and you can't even age it in this weather. What the hell were you thinking?"

"Roger hit it with the truck, and we didn't want it to suffer," one of the guys said. (I figured he was lying.)

Harry and I paused long enough to get the drift of the matter. These two guys had been out jacklighting, and now they needed to get this deer cleaned up quick before it spoiled, or before they got caught. I could hear Uncle Jake's bandsaw going, and the buzz, buzz, buzz of steaks being cut off.

"Well, at least make yourselves helpful and wrap this stuff up. The butcher paper is over there."

Uncle Jake would help anyone, especially if there was something in it for him. He'd probably get a few steaks, or a favor sometime. He was a pretty good man, but he knew how to make the most of a deal. That was how, he said, he stayed in business. He was an opportunist in every sense of the word. I could see sawdust being tossed on the floor, bits of it drifting out the door into the light. It was obvious that Jake was in control of the situation and would take care of these guys and their ill-gotten game.

We drifted away down the street, past the bar with the long-timers – the ones who would be there nightly until closing, the lonely ones, maybe without a family, or maybe with a family they wished they didn't have. They were all longing for a different life, something other than a small-town mill worker's life.

I thought about Uncle Jake. He seemed like a good guy. Grandpa Harry said that he used to be happy-go-lucky, but after he got married to Betty he changed. Aunt Betty had a hard edge. You could feel it right away. If you were well-to-do she was sweet as sugar, and when people went into the market she was very nice, but you knew she had a really hard side, and you didn't want to cross her. Jake started to be more concerned about money once they were married. They opened up the shop and had to scrape to get by for a while, but once they started to turn a profit, they never looked back. The money kept rolling in, but they continued to scrimp. They didn't need to anymore, but I guess it just became a habit. They were planning to put their daughter through college, even though she seemed to want only to settle down and get married when she got out of high school. Their son was destined to take over the shop even though he hated being there because his mother was so mean to him, always making him feel as though he couldn't do anything right. That Aunt Betty was a hard one for sure, but I think it was her upbringing. I think she'd had it hard too, and her parents were poor, and in a big family she'd never had anything of her own and had always been at the bottom of the pecking order. Well, it just trickled down to my cousin Clyde, their son. Clyde was a lot like his dad, an easygoing jester. Betty hated this about him and wanted him to take the store responsibilities more seriously, to step up to the plate and fill in for Jake. Instead Clyde would slip out for a cigarette or a sip of whiskey, sometimes not coming back until the family was asleep. Betty would be riding his tail the whole next day, but that only caused him to find other escapes.

As we were climbing the hill up to the farm we passed a hobo walking towards town. You could always tell a hobo; they always seemed to have more clothes on than the weather required, except in the winter. I had seen this guy before. He had a slight limp, was unshaven and wore what looked like corduroy pants, three flannel shirts, and a hat pulled down over his eyes. He had a knapsack on his back with a tin cup dangling from it. He was carrying bags too, two flour sacks joined by a rope and slung over his shoulder. He jangled as he walked, so you knew there were other items of importance to him that were hidden somewhere on his person or in a bag. As a rule hobos were pretty quiet, but this one talked to himself as he walked.

"Damned sheriff. I wasn't even close to that train. Can't a man walk innocently down by the tracks without being accosted? My mother would have given him a lick or two... Gonna run me out of town? I've seen him going down there himself, and him acting all self-righteous... Damned lawmen. Who are they working for, anyway?... Who do they think pays their salary?... Who are they protecting, anyway? Why, I coulda been killed! Why didn't they come to help me?"

We could hear him going on, his voice gradually getting fainter as he got farther away. He was one of a strange and independent lot. When given the choice they preferred to wander, never staying long in one place. This guy – we called him Old Samuel – favored the railroad tracks, and he would do odd jobs in town for a meal or a warm corner in a warehouse or shop. He was meticulous. When he was given a job to clean something, it would be spotless when he was done. He was honest to a fault. People would let him sleep in a shop after he cleaned the floor or washed the windows, and he never touched a thing. But he didn't like kids much, and he preferred to work either for people who didn't have them or in a place where he could be apart from them. I heard that he had lost his family, a wife and two kids, when a truck hit their car on a bad curve up on the hill and pushed it into the river. He lived, but he couldn't save them, and he hadn't ridden in a car since. He had a slight limp we heard was caused by a rail-yard dog, and we sometimes heard him muttering about the "bone polisher what caused it."

Some of the hobos around town were just old bums out to get a drink or a cigarette or a coffee. Matilda always gave them a meal when they came around, but never anything more. She said she didn't want to contribute to their "downfall." I think she had a reputation amongst these tramps as the milk lady because that would be what they asked for when they stopped by. She once pointed out the chalk mark at the end of our road that signaled to the other hobos that a kind woman lived down there. She would always give them some milk, and a plate of whatever we were having for dinner, or a sandwich. Sometimes she would let them sleep in the barn; she had one of them cleaning it out for a while until he disappeared. They never seemed to be able to stay in one place for long. That was something that they all had in common: they were restless wanderers. That's what Harry said. People who had too many hard knocks in life, people who were too sensitive, too tender. These people couldn't hold up under life's pressures by themselves, so they escaped and kept on wandering until they wore themselves out. I saw it happen to a sick groundhog once. He walked round and round in a circle, the same circle. Hours later when I passed him again, the circle was bloody from his worn-out paws. Finally his body just gave up, and he dropped over.

That's why, Harry said, you had to get some character. Don't be afraid of hard work, and find a life mate who will stay with you, one you'll want to be with for the rest of your life. Then, when the times get tough, you have someone to fall back on, and you'll have someone you can help when they're having a hard time too.

Chapter 10

The Tutor

A new school year was always exciting for me. Matilda and Harry would bring me to Norwich and buy me a new pair of shoes, several shirts, pants, socks, and sometimes a jacket. A binder and paper, pen, ink and pencils, a pencil sharpener and an eraser rounded out the spending spree.

I started to think about Rachael. When I imagined what love was about, I would think of Rachael. She was beautiful. She had shining dark hair and deep dark eyes. She wasn't silly and giggly like the other girls. And there were times I looked at her that I got this powerful feeling in my chest, like an aching. School was still a little ways off, but I was starting to hatch a plan that might bring us closer together.

I knew Rachael was a good student and that the teachers neither favored nor ignored her, but the one subject she had trouble with was math. I decided to take on Rachael's math tutelage as a personal task. I knew we would have to do some backtracking to give her a good foundation. Then she would be able to keep up with the class. At the beginning of the school year I approached her. She was shy, almost mute, but I knew she liked me because I would catch her stealing glances at me when she thought I wasn't looking. When I offered to help her she declined at first, but with my gentle persistence, and after I clearly laid out my plan, she finally said she would talk to her parents about it. I told her we could study in the library or at the farm.

I knew she wasn't talking to her parents – Harry had told me that it was primarily her grandmother who was raising her – but by the next Monday she said we could do it. That afternoon when school let out we went to the library and sat down next to each other, and there I started on a very pleasurable task. I had saved an apple, and when I took it out and cleft it in half with my pocket knife, the lesson in fractions began. I found her apt, and when presented with a problem that could be illustrated or worked through in steps, she was able to grasp the concepts. She was interested in the hows and whys of problems and this helped her understanding.

We met three times a week for the first few weeks, but then had to cut back to twice a week at her insistence. She was a great student, and she had her numbers down so well that we only had to work on concepts. As it started to get colder out, and it seemed as though she wouldn't need much more tutoring, I became more nervous about losing my pupil altogether. I would find more advanced work for her, trying to make it worthwhile so that we could continue. All the while we had been working together I would talk about Harry and Matilda, and later I would talk about my father and mother. Talking of my parents and their tribulations seemed to make her feel more comfortable talking about her own situation, and when I told her that I knew she lived with her grandmother, she looked relieved that perhaps I understood. She wouldn't have to explain further or otherwise pretend. With family situations somewhat similar, we felt a bond and became fast friends. The kids at school, who at first had teased me, began to leave me alone, seeing we were actually working on schoolwork and that Rachael was indeed improving.

The only person who was trouble was Kevin. I never forgot or forgave him after that first encounter that got me into so much trouble. He was sweet on Rachael too, and he didn't at all like it that I had been allowed the favor of tutoring her. He wasn't good in math – or anything else but whacking cats - so he didn't have any idea how to approach her except in his generally crude way.

Rachael didn't have a boyfriend. She seemed too innocent to have one, and she certainly wasn't interested in Kevin. When she told him so, he humiliated her in front of all the kids at school by exposing her mother as one of the prostitutes. This caused a big brouhaha, and the nuns tried to get Rachael taken away from Lily and put into a home for wayward girls. When the time came for the court hearing, Rachael's mother showed up. Lily was dignified and proud and determined to keep her daughter. She was not the downtrodden trollop the nuns were expecting, someone they thought they would be able to bully into giving up her child. Lily stood right there and countered each of their allegations. Rachael was clean and neat and respectful. She studied hard and got good grades. Lily went on, and then pointed out how the police chief personally gave her pointers in ethics, and that the judge himself (the one presiding over the hearing) had given her some grammar tutoring. This caused such a ruckus that the judge dismissed the case. He had determined that as far as he could see the girl was doing fine, and that her mother's lifestyle, which in his judgment had not been proven, did not seem detrimental to the child's upbringing, and besides, she was being brought up by her grandmother. Whack! Case dismissed! Of course the nuns were stunned by this sudden turn of events, but they saw that it would be to their advantage to let this little fish go. Who knew how deep Lily's affiliations went?

The townsfolk were divided on it all. Most of them seemed not to care since it didn't affect them. Maybe a husband or two would get home late on a Friday night, or go fishing until dusk on Saturday, but their wives generally turned a blind eye. They weren't bringing home any disease, or asking for divorces, or annoying them much in other ways, so they just let it be. A few of those who were steady churchgoers were indignant. Many of them were no saints either, and the loudest ones were the biggest hypocrites without so much as a real Christian bone in their whole body. So people watched while they wagged their tongues, but then they turned away.

One of the loudest in protesting Lily and Rachael was Lucille Hunt. No one could understand this because Buck, her husband, was not only a mean and nasty man, but he himself was known to climb the path to Jenny's Way. But Lucille would go on and on to anyone who would listen about how the camp on Jenny's Way was the blight of the town and the moral morass snaring the men. Lucille, miserable in her own life, was on a mission. She couldn't control her husband or son, but she would show this town that her little family wasn't as morally bereft as some of the others, especially Jenny and Lily, who acted like they were better than she was. She'd show them.

Chapter 11

First Visit

When Rachael finally invited me up to the camp, my imaginings of a wild orgy with fishermen clothed only in their fly-fishing hats and naked girls and red velveteen curtains was dashed.

There were two routes to the cottages. The actual Jenny's Way was a dirt road that entered from Pautipaug Hill Road off of West Main Street. This dropped steeply into the ravine and connected at the cottages with another path that the fishermen used. The fishermen's path entered by the dam and ran along the lake edge. The quickest route for me to get to Jenny and Rachael's was by the fishermen's path following the lake edge. That's the one we took. It was also the one that Gerry and I met up with Buck on and where after haying we saw the couple by the water. It was well-worn but not wide enough to drive on. Rachael said that lots of her mom's friends came by boat.

Rachael and I walked up the path, past my fishing holes. I pointed out the different places where my buddies and I swam and fished and she nodded and said she knew people used those spots but that her grandmother told her to stay clear of them, that you never could tell what kinds of people might be down there. This made me snigger under my breath and Rachael turned and looked at me disapprovingly. "So you think that fishermen and kids swimming are innocent and that people at Jenny's Way are somehow not as good? Not as trustworthy? Do you think somehow you're better?" Rachael's eyes flashed a challenge at me, her normally gentle and serene façade showing a moment of testy passion.

"Um, no, I don't think that." I was trying to figure out how to answer. "I think you are every bit as good as me. I'm not judging you or anyone." I was hoping this would satisfy her and we could move on. She still stood facing me with one hand on her hip, the other holding her books. I followed up, "You know I respect you. Look at me. I'm just a farmer. I couldn't judge anyone." I don't know why I came up with the farmer remark, but it seemed to satisfy her. She nodded, said okay, and turned back up the path. I walked quickly to catch up to her and walk by her side in the narrow lane.

I think I was just so excited to be visiting the camp for the first time that I wasn't thinking clearly. I was going to see where Rachael lived, meet her grandmother and maybe her mother, and see the camp that Harry talked about. Since we'd first seen the guys going down the road and then the couple by the water, my mind had replayed the scenes and my imagination tried to fill in the details. Harry's confirmation of what seemed like wild imaginings only made me more curious and anxious on this first visit.

I hadn't told my buddies about it. I was afraid they would follow us. I did tell Harry and Matilda because I didn't want them to worry, but mostly because I wanted them to give me an okay, to show their acceptance of my continued tutoring now at the camp. My mind was swimming. I was on the path with Rachael, alone, walking side by side, going to her house, and I was thinking of Buck, and my buddies, and Harry and Matilda. We rounded the last bend in the shore where the hills started to close in, almost making a ravine, and she turned slowly up the hill. It wasn't until we started that ascent that all these thoughts went away and I was in the moment with Rachael as she started to describe who lived where and the dynamics of the camp and her family.

Rachael explained that Lily was very protective of her, always fearful that she might someday follow in her footsteps. Lily was a product of her upbringing, and as much as Jenny tried to keep her out of it, the close association and the easy, pleasant and often professional clientele drew her in. To protect Rachael, Lily set her up with Jenny in the last cottage at the camp.

We ascended the well-worn path through the cool hemlocks on the north side. Tired tree roots held puddles of green moss and smooth rocks punctuated the ferns among haphazard clumps of wildflowers. Rachael said that in the summer it became a cool and inviting glade, with the lake below and the gentle sound of the water lapping at the shore where bathers washed and cooled off on those hot days.

The path rose gently, then leveled out and forked where a dirt road ascended the hill, soon giving way to a slightly widened area where the first of the four cottages nestled into the hill. The first cottage sat on the path to the left of the dirt road, and the others on the path to the right. This first one was where Jenny originally lived after leaving her husband. Now Sharon's, it was small and rough, but visitors could see it was clean and comfortable if not rich or fancy. Rachael knocked. No one answered, and we stepped in. It had two windows in the front, one set over the table in what served as the kitchen. A small wood stove squatted right in the middle. To the left of the stove a thin partition with a curtain door split off the kitchen and living area from the bedroom. The kitchen had some shelves lined with a few canned goods, and a couple of pots and pans hung from the wall. The table was enamel, three wooden chairs painted bright red with flower decals on their backs. A kerosene lamp hung over it, and on it lay a deck of cards and an ashtray. The bedroom had a window in the front too, and a metal frame bed with metal springs and a stuffed cotton mattress. Clothes hung from wall hooks, and a simple set of drawers served as a dresser, over which hung a small tarnished mirror. Several perfume bottles stood on the dresser beside a basin, some hankies, and a tortoise-shell comb and brush set. Attached to the wall was a candle in a holder, with a picture tacked next to it. A worn braided rug covered some of the floor. Outside the door, on a rough bench, rested a washtub, a washboard, and a chair.

As we passed the cottages Rachael introduced them. The second cottage on the right fork and above the path was Emma and Linda's, then came Lily's. Jenny and Rachael lived in the last and biggest cottage on the path, a little higher up. Saying that Jenny called them "her girls," Rachael smiled at me and cast her eyes down demurely.

All the cottages looked out over the lake and from their porches you could see the blinding sparkle of the setting sun shining off the water.

Rachael stepped through Jenny's screen door and spoke quietly to someone as I stood on the porch. Then she opened the door, pulled me in and introduced me. "Gram, this is John E. He's the one who's been tutoring me." I stepped in and shyly put my hand out to Jenny. She took it and then put her other hand over it, looking intently into my face.

"Good to meet you, John E. I've been hearing a lot about you." I was surprised at how warm and firm her hands were and although they looked worn and wrinkled, they felt soft. She looked directly into my eyes and her blue eyes crinkled at the corners as she smiled. I felt a sense of calm, of welcome. It's hard to explain and I would never tell my buddies but she made me feel like I belonged, all in that short hello and handshake. "Put down your books. Sit down. Would you like some soup? Tea? I think we even have some soda, but it might not be very cold."

Rachael put her books on the table and mine too as I replied, "Ah, sure, I'll have a little soup." She set the table with three large mugs and two plates from the shelf, then reached into a wooden box for half a loaf of bread and started slicing it, putting a couple slices on each plate. A small crock of butter and a knife appeared. "Sit down," she said, pushing me towards one of the chairs. Jenny ladled soup into our mugs and a little into a mug for herself. We all sat down to pea soup and bread.

As we ate and talked, I looked around Jenny's cottage. It had a real brick chimney, set up for a wood-fired kitchen stove. Although the stove was small it looked big in this cottage. Jenny said she always had something good on it, and she would feed anyone who showed up at the door hungry. She had a kitchen table snuggled up against the wall under the front window to take advantage of the light. It had four chairs, two each on opposite sides of the table, and a nail barrel on the end that she used as a stool. Everyone in the camp knew to come in on their own and help themselves. Sometimes one or more of the camp girls would come up for lunch or dinner and bring one of their fellas. Jenny always had enough food for all, and almost everyone stopped in early in the morning for coffee and toast or eggs or soup— whatever was on the stove. That stove was a great thing, especially in the winter, but in the summer she used a little kerosene stove out on the modest front porch. There were more or less two bedrooms. Jenny's had a blanket over the doorway of her tiny alcove, but Rachael's room, though small, had a proper door. There was also a small bed set sideways against the wall of the living area, and with pillows propped against the wall it served as a couch. I noticed one of the pillows looked satiny; it was red-fringed, with a picture of pine trees and a canoe, and "Lake George" printed on it in fancy script. A small shelf that hung on the wall held a dictionary and a few favorite books, even a Bible.

Jenny said that kitchen was where all the living happened. The stove concealed a reservoir that kept water warm all day and night. The fellas who visited would be required to do chores as part of their payment to the girls, and hauling water up from the lake was one of them. They would carry a pail or two and empty them into the rain barrel on the corner of Jenny's cottage. She would go out and draw a bucket off and fill her reservoir on the stove. She always had a big kettle on it ready for a hot cup of tea beside the aluminum percolator prepared for coffee requests. The fellas would also bring wood and split it for the stove, leaving it piled on the porch.

Once we finished our soup Rachael and I opened our books to study, while Jenny took our mugs and plates and washed them in a bucket on the porch.

We heard a shriek, then laughter, then a screen door slamming, and we knew people were moving about.

I was at Jenny's Way, sitting and having soup and tea with Jenny and Rachael. How I would love to tell my buddies if I could, but I knew that wasn't a possibility. I was now part of the camp, and if I started telling tales, true or not, I wouldn't be welcome back here. No one said it but I knew it was part of an unspoken code. And I wanted to come back.

Chapter 12

Sharon

I gradually learned the history of the camp. Every cottage after Sharon's was a little bigger than the previous one. All nestled about twenty yards apart, each one almost out of view and earshot of the adjacent ones. None were grand, and all looked as though they were built from leftovers at the lumberyard and hardware store. Nothing matched. No two windows were alike. Some were roofed with flattened oil cans, and most had several shades of asphalt shingles. Even though the cottages were rough and poor, they looked lived in, warm, comfortable, and inviting. You just knew that here no one was going to holler at you for walking in with dirty shoes or hay in your hair. You felt as though you were always welcome. You could relax.

The smallest cottage, the first on the left, where Jenny had first lived, was Sharon's. Sharon was the newest girl, tall, with thick curly blonde hair, buxom, and what was politely called "big-boned". The first time I saw her we were studying at Jenny's when she came bursting in, dragging a fella by the hand, laughing and loudly asking Jenny, "Hey, I'm all out of rubbers. You got any?" Jenny gave her a look that said it all; wide-eyed she put an index finger up to her lips. Sharon turned sharply and saw Rachael and me. "Oh, geeze, I'm sorry. I didn't know you were here! I'm so sorry to disturb you." She backed out as Jenny discreetly handed her the rubber.

Sharon oozed sensuousness and fun. Rachael told me later that she had fallen on hard times when the guy she was seeing got her pregnant, and her mother threw her out. The guy was married and didn't want her with a baby. She ran away to the camp, and when the baby came she gave him to the nuns. She left him on the doorstep and ran away. Jenny said it was a warm morning when Sharon walked down from the camp early, before it was light, and came back empty-handed and bawling. She knew that she couldn't care for this baby. She didn't have a job and didn't feel right keeping the baby at the camp. Part of her wanted to be young and free and to enjoy life unencumbered. Another part wanted to keep this wee little thing. She still loved the man, but he had jilted her as soon as he found out. She was alone and hurting and a baby carried too much responsibility for a young woman. The rest of the girls up Jenny's Way were accepting and caring, knowing all too well the fickleness of men and the occasional sting from being used and then discarded. They took her in and didn't ask questions. She bunked with Lily while she was pregnant and for a while afterward. She wasn't pressed to join the trade; she just became part of the family. Then one day, while she and one of the fishermen were joking over a beer, well, she just fell into it. Now she was comfortable in the first cottage and conducted a fair share of business there.

There had been a few other girls who came and went, from what Rachael could make out maybe a half dozen, but now the camp had settled down to a small but comfortable group who seemed like family.

The men who visited the camp were thoughtful and decent– Jenny insisted on it. They were primarily regulars, but when someone new came Jenny would have a beer with him and find out what his disposition was. Rachael said that Jenny had an uncanny intuition about people. If she didn't like him he wasn't invited to stay. This pretty much served to keep the men in a polite mood, and it was small payment for the fun at the camp. Most of the fellas would bring stuff: food, chocolate, wood, trinkets, sometimes clothes or perfume, or flowers, or beer. One of the fellas worked at the icehouse and would regularly bring up a block for Jenny's icebox. A gesture like this put them in good standing, but it also kept their bills low, since the girls didn't have to go to town if all their needs were provided for at home. It seemed like a pretty good trade for everyone.

Jenny loved her girls and kept them safe from rough characters. She also made sure they used protection and everyone was clean and didn't have any "dis-eases." She said she couldn't afford to be sending people to the hospital when all they had to do was keep to a few the rules.

From Friday afternoon after the mill workers got their pay until sometimes late that night, a small but steady stream of fellas would navigate their way up and down the path or road or come by boat. Seen from Sharon's cottage, the occasional flashlight or lantern light bobbed up and down the path in front of a guy traipsing along in the dark. At times the small dock below Sharon's had four or five boats tied to it. One afternoon someone brought an old crank Victrola up to Sharon's, and pretty soon everyone was out on the path, bouncing up and down and clapping to the rhythm of Count Basie.

After that, impromptu dancing would flare up like a wildfire on almost any afternoon.

Some of the fellas just hung around at Jenny's, having a beer and playing a few hands of poker or checkers or jumping into the lake if it had been a hot day. There'd be eight or ten guys sitting on Jenny's porch, in chairs or dangling their feet off or leaning up against the post and smoking a pipe. Some were even there fishing, and would hike back up the path with a couple of trout that Jenny would put right in the pan for them with a few onions.

Although it looked like a lake it was the water for the mill, and on some days in the summer the level would drop when the mill needed the power, but once the gates were closed it filled quickly. The Shetucket after all was a good river with strong flow, and the lake was always drifting towards the dam.

Jenny's stove was a beautiful piece of ironwork, all black cast iron and silver filigree. It was the heart of the camp, with its simmering water and stoked fire. Jenny named it Bertha. I occasionally had the privilege of chopping wood for it. Jenny knew I had a knack for splitting up firewood just the right size for her cook stove, and she often pressed me into service chopping up a small boxful. Jenny could do wonders with it: stovetop biscuits in a pan she would cover and then flip, roasts, and breads, and of course the ever-simmering soups. This went on from early fall into late spring, until it got too hot to have Bertha belching smoke and sparks. Then she would be put to bed for the summer, cleaned out and shined up, waiting for those first chilly fall days when the guys would enjoy bringing up the kindling again. The magic stove was always able to feed and warm anyone who came through the door.

One winter, a real bad cold snap and then a blizzard on top of it sent all the girls climbing through the snow up to Jenny's. She kept Bertha going, melting snow for water, stoking the fire all night long, and drawing the mattresses up so all the girls could sleep close to the stove. Jenny said they damned near went stir crazy playing cards and smoking cigarettes and drinking coffee, until finally the weather broke, and everything started to melt. Luckily they had brought in a big stack of firewood when it first got cold and stacked more by the door outside, or they would have had to dig it out of the snow pile that was up to the window. A couple of the fellas skied up the lake and dug them out. They received a very grateful welcome for their troubles.

Chapter 13

An Unexpected Meeting

Walking down the path to the camp on my next Saturday off, I was half daydreaming and half enjoying the beautiful day when down the road I saw two figures coming towards me, arm in arm. As I had become wary of those I met on the path, I stepped into the bushes before they saw me and waited for them to pass. As they came closer I could see the long black robes of what I could only imagine was a nun. It was Jenny and Sister Margaret, arm in arm, talking and laughing together. I held my breath until I thought I would burst. I could see Sister Margaret's habit, grey dust clinging to the hem, the beads and crucifix swaying as the women strolled down the road. I could hear them talking about one of the guys up at the camp and laughing as if they were very amused.

Once they were out of sight I ran up the path. When I got to Jenny's I had to lean on the porch post just to catch my breath. Lily and Rachael were having coffee, and both stared at me through the screen door. They asked me in, and I sputtered out what I had seen on the path.

Lily started to explain the startling sight. "Margaret and Jenny are sisters—real sisters. Margaret comes up to visit Jenny now and then to share the news about their mom and the goings-on around town." It turned out that their dad had died some years before and their mom was in failing health and went into the convent's old-age home. There Margaret ensured that she was well cared for, and Jenny didn't have to worry. As poorly as her mom and dad had treated Jenny, she still loved them and wanted her mom to be taken care of.

She even sent a few dollars her mother's way when she could spare it. Of course it didn't hurt to have Sister Margaret in her court on the issue of Rachael and her upbringing, even though she stayed out of the fray as much as possible.

Jenny rarely went to town to visit with Margaret, though. The only time the girls remembered seeing them together recently was at their father's funeral. But Margaret came up to the camp occasionally, and they had tea or lunch and chewed the fat for hours.

Jenny had said that Margaret was a true believer. Even as a child she used to go into raptures during the Mass when they would hold up the host and the chalice. Although she had been no goodie-two-shoes, according to Jenny, and had gotten into her share of mischief in school and at home, no one had been surprised when she had chosen to go into the convent after high school.

This whole story was surprising at first, but then as I began to settle into it I could see the similarities: the same crinkle around the eyes when they smiled, the same pairing of bluntness with underlying caring and generosity, the same integrity, and the same strong personality that drew people to both of them and made people feel safe. These two sisters found that their paths had led to different sides of the tracks, but they were able to bridge the gulf and remain close and caring. I would never be able to view Sister Margaret the same. I didn't lose respect for her but rather gained it. I would never view Jenny the same either. I would not be able to look at her without thinking of the sacrifices that she had made in order to save her daughter. I thought about the paths we take in life and wondered how we decide that one is right for us. Could we ever trace that path back and take the other turn, or was it lost to us forever?

Chapter 14

Camp Life

After the set-to with Lucille Hunt over Rachael, I was invited up to the camp to continue tutoring. Although we had gotten to a point where Rachael truly didn't need my help any further, I think Lily wanted her to have a regular friend. Spring was just around the corner, and the path to the camp was slippery and at times almost scary, but there were usually enough saplings to hold onto as I hiked up. Jenny's cottage was very inviting, with good smells and a fire in Bertha and the warm yellow glow of the ever-lit kerosene lamp hanging over the kitchen table. Jenny offered us some soup and biscuits and tea, all of which we gratefully accepted. We sat across from each other to study, and every once in a while Rachael would come around the table with her book and point to a particularly difficult spot in an equation that I would then try to explain. Then she would go back and work through it. This had gone on for about an hour when I had to leave. As I was putting on my jacket, Jenny spoke.

"Tell Harry I said hi, and Matilda too. I always liked them folks. They are good honest people. None better. You don't know how lucky you are to have wound up with them. You could still be with Mary."

I was surprised not only by what she knew about me but also by how frank she was about it. A little stirring of loyalty welled up in me. After all, it was my mother she was talking about, no matter how true.

"Yes, ma'am," was all I could muster. I went down the path pondering this. Yes, my mother was all about herself. Yes, my grandparents were good people. I often forgot my family situation, not even remembering most of the time that Harry and Matilda were my grandparents; they felt like father and mother. I was getting more of a taste of how strange the world really is.

When I told Harry what Jenny had said, he just shook his head.

"You know, I like Jenny, but sometimes she's just too blunt. The next time you see her you tell her I said hi back. And I want you to know that I don't mind you going up there, but I would take a little care not to be too obvious about it. People watch, and people talk, and a few people don't think much of the girls at the camp and wouldn't mind seeing them go away. Personally I've never seen much trouble in it. They're clean and honest, and they would have disappeared long ago if there wasn't any business for them. So I guess you see that there must be a need. I think most of the women those men leave at home are kinda relieved their husbands go out fishing now and then. It takes a little pressure off them, gives them a little free time. But I'm a one-woman man, and I'll tell you that's the best way to be. Once you find that woman, well, that's all you'll need in life; everything else will fall into place." It was another one of Harry's long but infrequent talks that gave me more to think about than I could handle in one evening.

The next time I visited the camp, spring had most certainly taken hold. Mud caked much of the path to it, and the north side still had frozen parts. Down by the lake the little blue hepatica and the yellow adder's tongue were blossoming. This Saturday morning Rachael and I were sitting at Jenny's kitchen table studying for a test. Suddenly we heard a screen door slam shut and saw a guy flash by running up the hill. Rachael giggled. I looked at her in surprise, because she didn't giggle all that much.

"That guy must have an emergency," she said, nodding her head towards the outhouse that was up the path a little ways.

It seemed that sometimes the guests would whoop it up a little too much on Friday nights, and some of the girls would let them sleep it off on the floor.

At that point Lily came in, looking relaxed in a kimono-like robe, and went to the stove to fix a cup of coffee. Smiling at us she sat down and took a long sip. "John E., it seems like your uncle can't hold his liquor."

My mouth must have gaped open.

Lily responded, "Don't look so surprised, little Johnny. You know Betty is no easy woman to spend— well, quality time with."

Always so delicate, these women; while willing to tell it like it was, they spelled it out gently. Yes, Aunt Betty was no prize, but what about what Harry said? What about the "one woman forever and ever" idea? I was getting the picture that choosing wisely the first time around was a major factor in the satisfaction ratio.

Uncle Jake came staggering down the path and into the kitchen. He was looking pretty peaked, and he headed straight for Jenny's big enamel percolator. Once he'd had a swig and had steadied himself against the partition his color came back a little, and he was able to focus enough to see me sitting there with Rachael and Lily. Just then Jenny came out of the bedroom. It was getting crowded.

"Geeze, John E.! I didn't know you were here!"

Jake was torn between embarrassment and sickness. He took another sip of coffee, got a doomed look on his face, and rushed out the door. We could hear him throwing up what was left in him. He came back later, dressed and with his face washed and hair combed. "I don't know what I'm going to tell Betty. She'll think I died. I suppose I could tell her them Moulton boys shot another deer, and I had to dress it and get it into the freezer. But what if she went down to the shop?" Jake was thinking out loud and still kinda fuzzy.

"Whatever you do, John E., don't tell her you saw me here. I don't know what she would do." He was by now comfortable with me being here and seeing him, and he was just trying to figure out a plausible story.

Just then a man came up onto the porch and knocked on Jenny's door, peering in.

Lily walked over and opened the door. "Come on in, Sam. What'cha got there? Wow, that's nice. Thank you very much. Why don't you grab a cup of coffee and we'll go visit at my house."

Sam sheepishly laid the quarter wheel of cheese and dozen eggs on the cupboard. He filled a cup with coffee and several spoons of sugar and headed out the door. Lily followed him, winking at me on the way.

I got the feeling that these women didn't make a lot for a living, but they didn't seem to want for anything either. Their lives seemed comfortable, and without the same demands of the workaday world that most of us had.

Chapter 15

Emma and Linda

Harry understood my desire to visit Rachael at the camp. I would rush through my Saturday chores watering the cows and chickens and feeding them and cleaning out their pens. If I didn't have to work at the mill I'd ask him if I could go to visit Rachael, and he would always give me the same answer.

"Go clean up. You don't want anyone to see you with manure up to your knees. And be back by dark."

I'd clean up and run off to the camp. This particular day I brought my fishing pole. I knew it would be hard to get any private time with Rachael, but under the guise of fishing we could spend a little time visiting. I always felt comfortable at Jenny's but sometimes I just wanted to be away from the goings-on there, and almost always things were going on.

So I stopped at the old manure pile and scratched out a half dozen worms and put them in the coffee can I carried, along with a few hooks and lead sinkers. I slipped through the edge of town almost unnoticed, as it was early and only the milkman and newspaper delivery kids seemed to be out. I walked down the sidewalk through the duplexes that bordered the upper end of the river by the bridge. There the tarmac road ended and a sidewalk ran beside the boardinghouse, the men's club and the river, ending at the big granite steps that bordered the edge of the dam. Then the road to Jenny's became a narrow lane and gradually resolved to a path, wide in spots but narrowing further in as use was less frequent. This morning seemed to be more beautiful than ever, and I felt carefree and light-hearted. The air was fresh and cool. The sun was warm on my back, throwing my shadow in front of me as I strode jauntily with my fishing pole. I didn't remember growing, but my shadow loomed larger than I'd remembered, and the shoulders seemed a little wider. I attributed it to the extra length of early morning shadows.

Arriving at the camp I passed Sharon, who had clothespins in her mouth. She waved as she hung a few freshly washed towels and some underwear on the line beside the cottage. The little blaze under the big galvanized washtub was still smoldering.

Jenny was of course up and had the coffee brewing. I could see Rachael in the kitchen over the basin that served as a sink, throwing water on her face and wiping it off. She stood up and turned to look at me with a smile. My heart was singing. I could see Jenny, who turned from me to Rachael and back to me. I lifted the can of worms and announced to them both, "I thought I'd go fishing today. Want to go, Rachael?"

"Yes, that would be great. Okay with you, Gram?" Rachael looked to Jenny.

"Oh, yeah, just have some breakfast first." Jenny, who always wanted to be sure people were fed, pulled down the large black skillet and set it on the stove. As the coffee perked its rhythmic gurgle Jenny started to crack eggs into the skillet.

"I need some wood for the stove, John E. How about it?" Jenny knew I was always game to split a little wood. Around the west side of the cabin a small roof jutted out from the cottage where split and unsplit oak and maple were piled. Close to it was a stump with an axe in it where the splitting, and occasional beheading and cleaning of fish and game, was done. I wound up for a passing shot at a short oak log, split a good armload for Jenny and brought a few pieces into the kitchen, leaving the bulk in the woodbin on the porch. Jenny stoked up the fire. Soon the crackle of bacon and eggs livened the air, and a lean-to toaster was put into service on one of the burners. While Jenny cooked breakfast (what looked like breakfast for an army), Rachael was busy in her room getting dressed and combing her hair.

When Rachael and I sat down to eat, Emma and Linda showed up with milk and other provisions. Emma turned the toast over on the lean-to toaster, removed two slightly burned pieces and buttered them. Linda poured coffee. Jenny gave them each a plate and they helped themselves to the eggs and bacon without ceremony, then went outside and settled into the chairs, using the flat-topped woodbin for a table. I could hear them chatting about the previous night.

Jenny started to tell their story. "Now I don't want you to be to shocked, John E., but there are all kinds of people in the world. I'm gonna tell you about a couple of the nicest ones." And she went on to describe what Lily had told her about Emma and Linda.

"Those two showed up at Lily's one evening in a nasty thunderstorm, cold and wet. Rachael was a baby and still living with Lily. I was living in the first cottage up the right fork, where Emma and Linda live now. Lily was living in the first little cottage on the left, where Sharon lives. Since Lily's was the first cottage on the way, it was the one where they had knocked at the door and asked for shelter."

Jenny paused to move one of the cooktops and drop a couple pieces of wood into the stove.

"As Lily told it, Emma had her arm around Linda's shoulder. Linda, clutching a wool blanket over herself, was wet from head to foot and shivering. Lily had only a little kerosene heater at the time so she brought them up to my cottage, where a small wood stove was going. My kerosene lamp threw a warm circle over the kitchen table, and I watched them shivering and warming their hands by the stove. Emma shyly explained their situation, gulping the tea I'd given her, holding the cup with both hands for warmth.

"Emma told it this way: they had been friends since they were freshmen in high school, and they somehow managed to spend time together even when Linda started working part time at the mill. Emma would meet Linda at the mill and walk her home. Sometimes they'd stop for a malted at Lincoln's and sit in the booth and talk for hours. One day at Linda's front door Emma kissed Linda on the cheek. Linda was surprised but returned the kiss. The next day the same long walk, visit at Lincoln's and kiss on the cheek. Emma said that by the end of the next week she would also say 'Love you' before they parted. Then she ventured to kiss Linda on the lips. Linda pulled back, but still met her the next day. Eventually, step by step, Emma and Linda became lovers."

Jenny paused. "Now, John E., I know this is not something you're familiar with, but you've got to understand that love is love. It's not always what we're used to. It's just that there are all kinds of love. Do you understand?" I nodded, and she went on. "Well, one day Linda's parents discovered them and threw Linda out of the house. Of course Emma, who had a difficult family life, left home to be with Linda. They didn't know what to do or where to go. The first night they slept under the grandstands at the ballpark. They had only the clothes they were wearing and a blanket. It started to rain and they needed to find shelter, and that's when Emma remembered these cottages and they showed up at Lily's.

"Of course we took them in, and didn't ask any questions. We knew what it was like to be on the fringes of society, and we instinctively knew that these were good women. Emma immediately felt comfortable with us and our friends, and after a little while took to the situation. Eventually Linda got comfortable with it too. They developed their own following. And soon some of the boys were bringing up lumber and tar paper, and I had a new cottage that I moved into. It wasn't uncommon for us to rearrange sleeping quarters, and Emma and Linda got my old cottage. They were as happy as they could be there. The only agreement they had with everyone was that at the end of the day they would sleep together, alone. And we were all fine with that."

As I watched them on the porch from the window, I realized that I had learned more about love and sacrifice from these two women than I had from most of the people in the town. When Rachael and I finished our breakfast and headed for the lake, I was whistling all the way.

Chapter 16

Lily

As time went on I learned more about the camp and one day, as Lily's birthday neared, Jenny told me more about her. Lily was Jenny's only child. Where Jenny was fair with blue eyes, freckles in the summer and thick auburn hair, Lily was fair but without the freckles. She inherited the dark hair and eyes of her father, Lucky. Some said she was a haunting beauty in her youth, black Irish.

Jenny did business in the evening when Lily was sleeping, and once Lily was old enough she walked her to school every day and back again. Often Sally, the first of Jenny's "girls," would take Lily into town and get her an ice cream sundae, and then wander through the stores so she would become familiar with town life and not be too isolated.

Lily knew about the mills because some of her mother's "friends" worked there. She saw the rows of duplexes and asked questions about them, wondering why people would choose to live so close to one another and not up in the quiet woods with a serene lake at their doorstep.

She knew regular people worked but wasn't clear on how the girls survived at the camp except she could see food and beer and gifts come into the house regularly. But she never questioned it much. When she asked her mother where her father was, Jenny explained that he'd gone away but he sent his friends to help her take care of Lily.

On the occasions she had the opportunity to visit the home of a friend from school, she remarked not on the indoor plumbing or modern wringer washer but on the size and comfort of the large beds with thick puffy mattresses and luxurious linens.

As much as Jenny tried to protect Lily from the lifestyle she had grown into, her beauty was just too alluring and as dangerous as a dog in season. Sweet young men swarmed around their cottage bringing gifts and flowers and candy. Finally Lily found one too delicious to resist and when Jenny was busy, slipped away for an evening. Jenny was beside herself when she realized Lily was missing, but in some way felt that this may have been inevitable. Lily had made it through eighth grade and a couple years of high school, and she was filling out and looking like a woman. When she showed up with the boy in tow, Jenny told him he'd have to marry Lily and make her an honest woman. Jenny liked the boy. He was good-looking, clean and well-mannered. Jenny thought Lily might find her way out of the camp, perhaps even into a good family. The boy promised he would marry her, but no plans were ever made, and he continued to visit and take Lily out for a stroll until she got pregnant. Then he stopped visiting and Lily was heartbroken. She moped around the camp for months, everyone trying to cheer her without success. Some of the regular fellas said they didn't recognize him as a millworker. They tried to find him, but he seemed to have left town. Lily had a rough winter, pregnant and unable to get out much, but fortunately there was little snow.

In the spring Rachael came and Lily was in love again. Lily adored Rachael, who Jenny said was the spitting image of Lily as a baby. She carried her everywhere, showing her the lake, the fish, the turtles the flowers, the birds. She borrowed one of the boats and paddled Rachael up and down the lake talking to her about the cottages and boats and boys. Rachael couldn't understand a thing, but listened and talked baby talk back to Lily. Rachael blossomed. Lily and Rachael were living with Jenny, and after a time Lily took on the business. Once she did, and Jenny couldn't talk her out of it, Jenny insisted that she be allowed to take care of Rachael. Lily could see the sense of this and moved in with Sharon for a while until another cottage was built.

Chapter 17

A New Cottage

The next day when I visited, Jenny continued to describe the evolution of the camp.

By the time Emma and Linda had settled in there were three cottages. The first one on the left was originally Sharon's, and then Lily moved in. Lily liked knowing who was coming up to the camp, and from there she could keep her eye on things. When she wasn't busy she would sit out in front with the fellow, offer him a beer and chew the fat, learning the latest goings-on in town and sharing what she'd heard from the previous guy. The camp had more up-to-date news than the local paper. Sharon would sometimes entertain when Lily was on the porch or occasionally ask Lily to see what Jenny was up to. There were times too when Sharon just brought her friend down to the lake to "cool off."

Emma and Linda's cottage was next, first on the right fork, and Jenny's was the farthest up. When Rachael came along some of the fellas got together and built one last cottage on the path, the finest one.

Jenny described the building of the newest cottage. It started when Jimmy from the lumberyard drove his pickup down the dirt road as far as he could go and came running down the path looking for volunteers. He didn't say why, but when he was able to get three other guys they started carrying bricks and beams and 2x8s down the hill, and finally they lugged pieces of an old used cook stove. They even brought some of it in by boat. Jimmy threw a tarp over it all and went to Jenny.

"I got a deal on a pile of lumber. They were going to get rid of it, and I volunteered to help clean out the old stock if they would let me have it. They were most agreeable. Some of us guys thought you might like another cottage. What do you think?"

Jenny was so thrilled she couldn't speak. She pointed up the path far enough past the last cottage to where it leveled off in a little plateau, so the new one would be out of sight in the summer.

Jimmy came by the next weekend with more materials. He and several others started the work by digging seven holes: four where the corners would be, two between them for extra support, and a seventh, larger one in the center. The six outside holes he lined with stone and finally topped with brick. The seventh he made wider, lined it with stone and topped it with mortar and brick. This was a large rectangular hearth to set the cook stove on and a brick chimney to come up behind it.

He had some of the other guys cutting the 2x8s to the proper length, hand saws going to and fro. It was a busy work site. They framed out the floor and put a layer of one-inch pine on it, and even got the framed walls up before they had to quit because darkness was falling. With a window in the front facing the river and path, another one in the side facing the other cottage, and a small one in the back, it felt like a palace. Jenny and Lily went up there in the dark and sat in the front door opening, the frame of roof and walls open to the trees and sky. Sharing a cigarette, they luxuriated in their good fortune.

Jimmy and the guys toiled hard in the heat. After working up a serious sweat they went down to the lake for a dip, then came back up for the beers and ham sandwiches that Jenny and some of the other guys had provided. This whole time the camp was buzzing. Everyone knew what was happening, and most of the regulars took as much time as they could to come up to the camp and be part of the project. Those who had no carpentry skills carried lumber or brought a keg of nails or extra beer. Someone smacked his thumb and ended up with a black fingernail, and all the other guys teased him about his aim. Lily stuck up for him, joking that his aim was JUST fine.

In a few more days additional materials came. Jimmy, true to his word, had a roof up in three weeks and a brick chimney pushing through it. Then a tin roof was made of mismatched pieces of metal, but it was water-tight. He flashed the chimney, and when he could get five other guys they carried the main body of the cook stove up to the cottage from the bottom of the path where they had unloaded it from the truck. They rested frequently. They carried it through the door frame, which had remained incomplete due to the stove's size, and assembled it: a black cook stove with lime-green enamel accents. Although small, it took up the whole new hearth and commanded the center of the room.

Used but serviceable windows arrived that even had screens, and the real wooden door had a screen door too. In another week Jimmy got the cottage watertight and comfy and had some shelves and a room divider built, along with other details that added to the creature comforts.

An impromptu party followed the finishing touches, and everyone enjoyed hot dogs and beans and beer and ice cream. Then they helped to move Jenny's furniture and a few boxes of pots and dishes, cooking utensils, buckets, and some personal items from her old cottage up to this new "mansion."

Jenny was moved in and soon made this cottage the comfortable gathering place where we were having breakfast.

Chapter 18

Hannibal

Rachael and I were finally off to the lake. The water was high that day, but the cove where I liked to fish was quiet enough to see the bottom and a few fish lingering in the shadows.

We sat on the jutting piece of ledge. I baited my hook and threw it in, satisfied just to sit and gaze at Rachael in the dappled shadows cast by the soft green leaves of the overhanging birch. The birds were singing with a fury, flowers blossomed on the bank, and it was even more peaceful and beautiful than I had ever remembered.

When I looked at Rachael, her dark hair falling over her shoulders as she peered into the water, I felt stirrings that were not wholly unfamiliar, something more than the platonic love I'd been feeling. I had felt this briefly before, but now it was almost overpowering. I could barely contain my excitement. I wasn't sure what to do or how to handle this intense feeling. So I did what any stupid boy would do: I threw a big rock into the water right in front of her. She jumped back, gasping, wet and surprised. Much to her credit, instead of being angry she laughed, and cupping some water she splashed me back. The tension was broken, and as quick as that my fishing pole bent down into the water. I grabbed it and tried to set the hook. A battle ensued between me and a fairly decent-sized smallmouth bass. When I got it up to the edge of the rocks and was about to pull it up, it gave a last swish and spit the hook out. I was sort of relieved; I didn't know if I was prepared to be diverted by a fish.

I re-baited the hook, cast into a deeper spot by a sunken log, and settled in again. We started to talk about our families, the camp, all the characters we knew and their idiosyncrasies, and what a strange and wonderful world we lived in. We were deep into conversation when we heard a commotion coming from the dirt road above the camp. While normally we might hear people walking by and talking, this was the shouting of several voices, all sounding very excited. I pulled in my line and we went up to see what it was all about.

There on the dirt road, wobbling along, was a mattress, and under it were two guys struggling to stay on the path and keep the mattress out of the dirt. Behind them were several more guys with a box spring and behind them a guy with what was probably part of a bed frame. We ran up and asked if we could help. The guy with the frame pointed behind him and said there was a frame farther back down the path. I ran down and picked up a headboard, and Rachael picked up a piece of frame too. We all started down the path, the guys struggling to keep the mattress up, hooting and hollering and laughing all the way. This parade was a comic sight. Like Hannibal crossing the Alps, they struggled up the rough narrow path. Someone at the bottom hollered to stop, he had to rest. We all stopped, and they put down the mattress and box spring for a minute. There was much excited talking because they knew that this was a fine piece of furniture and it would be a happy woman who got it. The parade resumed, with more hooting, hollering, grunting, and groaning all the way. When we got within earshot of the first cottage, people started to appear. Soon a whole crowd gathered to see what was happening and help with carrying the goods to the camp.

It seemed that someone in town had bought this for Lily, although no name was mentioned. Lily thought she knew who it was but wasn't about to let on. Now some serious horse trading started among the girls. Lily had a comfortable but old double bed that she was going to pass on to someone. All the girls were animated, but it was obvious that Emma and Linda would probably get it. They had a very old cotton mattress with open springs below that squeaked when they moved on it. Sharon's cottage was too small for Lily's old bed. Jenny's wasn't that old, and she was satisfied with her single bed that gave her more room.

The guys all went to Emma and Linda's. They pulled the old bed out and set it up on Jenny's porch, and they moved Lily's old bed into the spot left empty. Emma and Linda were like kids, pulling out their second set of linens, making the bed and immediately falling upon it laughing.

Setting up the new bed at Lily's was a ritual of highest solemnity. The fellas were careful not to scratch anything or get the new mattress or box spring dirty. They leveled it and steadied it, checking it for sturdiness and stability. Then someone produced new linens. That just put Lily over the top, and she started to cry. It was a kind and generous gesture to a warm and caring woman. This beautiful new bed made the cottage look like what it was, a tiny cottage of poor mismatched materials, worn and rundown. I think we all were getting misty-eyed, and then Jenny offered up the standard beer and hot dogs and we all headed up there while Lily just sat on the bed smoothing the covers, saying she'd be along in a minute.

Jenny passed around beers and handed sodas to Rachael and me. Four of the guys plopped onto Emma and Linda's old bed on the porch, and a couple of them were making obscene movements amid lots of laughter. Jenny's porch was getting crowded, what with the bed, the water barrel, the wood box, the chairs, and the kerosene stove, but she didn't seem to care. She paid attention only to the hot dogs and beans she was warming up. We ate heartily and drank and laughed; everyone was in a spirited mood. A few more people arrived, and pretty soon Lily had the Victrola cranked up and playing a piano rag, and she was dancing around swishing a violet handkerchief through the air. A couple of guys started dancing around too, and Emma and Linda were soon in the fray with another guy. The rest of us sat there and laughed at them cavorting on the narrow path, jumping on and off the porch. It was a riotous sight. Someone was standing on the bed, then bouncing on it. Lily knocked one of the guys off the path with a hip swing, and he slipped down towards the lake a couple of yards before catching himself on a tree. Then they were prancing in a line, holding onto each other, through Jenny's house and back out and into Lily's, where the guys all decided to lift her up and set her down ceremoniously onto the new bed. A cheer went up, and several of them volunteered to break it in with her, but she pushed them off laughing and told them to wait until later. We were all in high spirits, thinking what a great time it was, unaware of what lay around the corner.

Chapter 19

Unexpected Turn

I headed towards home when the light got low, reluctant to leave the fun and silliness and Rachael behind, but I didn't want to make Harry or Matilda worry either.

Rachael walked me to the last cottage and, unexpectedly, kissed me on the cheek and then ran all the way back. I stood there watching her. I knew it for sure then. This was the one. There was no doubt in my mind; there never had been.

I wandered distractedly through the town, pausing to drop a quarter into Sarge's cup as I passed in front of the liquor store. Sarge was always stationed in front of the store. A veteran, he had no legs, but he sat his stumps on a small wooden platform with iron wheels, propelling himself along the sidewalk with little pegs held in his hands. He wore a short wool army jacket, and he would play the Battle Hymn of the Republic on his harmonica and salute everyone as they passed. Occasionally someone would drop him a coin for cigarettes or wine. No one knew where he lived, or if he had a family, but we suspected he slept in the package store some nights. He used to frighten me, but as I grew older I only felt sad for him. Tonight I was feeling very generous and dropped my quarter into his cup. I listened to the harmonica fading into the distance as I continued climbing the hill. I drifted into a dreamlike state, thinking about the kiss, thinking about the future. What would it bring?

Although I talked a little of Rachael to Harry and Matilda, I usually didn't give them a lot of details about the camp and the goings-on there. While I believed they were open-minded, there was an unspoken understanding that some things should be kept to myself. Besides, when I talked about Rachael, there was a certain tone, a reverence, which told them all they needed to know.

I went to bed with the day's events swirling around in my mind, always coming back to the same moments: when I looked at Rachael on the ledge at the lake, when I watched her run back after kissing me.

I didn't hear about that evening's events at the camp until the next morning when Sam stopped by for some eggs. I was out cleaning the cow stalls when he drove in. I could see him talking animatedly to Harry, his arms going this way and that. When I got out there I heard him say, "...and then he fell all the way down into the lake."

Harry turned to me and said, "There's been some trouble at the camp."

I couldn't get my pants changed fast enough.

Harry said he didn't think I should go, that I might not be able to get up there, but I couldn't help myself. I told him I would just get as close as I could and that I wouldn't get into any trouble.

I ran through the town. There were a number of people out in little groups, and where the dirt road started that went out to Jenny's Way a police car was parked, empty. I ran back down to the path by the dam. I saw a few people walking slowly back from the camp and one headed out there. I rushed by him and kept running. When I came up the path towards Sharon's cottage I could see the policemen, two of them, talking to Sharon. She looked as if she had a swollen bruise on her face and blood on her blouse. Jenny was sitting on Sharon's stoop. She was hunched over, looking small and old and tired. I sneaked up around the back of Sharon's, not wanting to be seen and stopped by the police. When I got to Lily's Rachael was there, and Lily and Emma too. Linda was up at Jenny's, trying to make coffee. They were all silent, looking down the hill towards Sharon's, and then they all started talking at once.

"It was Buck. You know, Jerome Hunt," Lily said. "He showed up at Sharon's last night. He would sometimes sneak up there because Jenny didn't like him and he didn't want her to see him. So he came up, but Sharon was busy. He'd had a few and started hollering, and then he went in and scared the guy off and started hitting Sharon. He was being the typical jerk that he was, screaming at the top of his lungs and saying awful things to Sharon. She was just crying while he was calling her a slut and asking her what does she think she's doing with these other guys. He went on and on. Well, Jenny could hear it from up at her cottage. She went into her wardrobe and took out the old double barrel she kept in there for emergencies. She loaded it with some old birdshot she had in the drawer and went down to scare Buck off. But he said he 'wasn't in the mood to be shagged off by some little old bitch.' And when he started to go towards Jenny, she just shot him. She said she didn't mean to, but he scared her and the gun just went off. He fell backward down the hill, glanced off a tree, and rolled into the lake. Everyone, all of us, just stood there watching; it all happened so fast. We didn't know what to do. None of us was about to go after him, and even if we could get him, he's such a big guy we wouldn't have been able to get him onto the bank. It's real steep right there on the edge, and besides, it was getting dark fast. He just floated down the lake. They found him this morning in the grate by the mill, where all the dead wood gets caught before it goes into the mill turbines. He was there amongst the driftwood and the leaves."

Lily went on. "We didn't know what to do. Should we tell the police or keep it quiet? But too many people knew. It was an accident. The police may not see it that way, though. Leave it to that damned Buck to mess up a good thing. So all the fellas left and some of them went to the police. They came running back up here last night with big flashlights, trying to find him on the bank, but it was just like we said: he was gone. There was some blood. I don't think Jenny killed him. She just winged him, but that sent him down into the lake, and he was pretty drunk anyway."

Everyone agreed, nodded, and had something to add. Sharon was a mess. Not only had her peaceful evening been shattered, but Buck, her old sweetheart, had beaten her up and then he had been shot right in front of her. She didn't love him anymore. She had finally found people to care for her here and to show her that she shouldn't be treated that way. Yet there was a bond. He'd come to her and be sweet, telling her how Lucille wasn't a good wife and didn't understand him and his needs, and then Sharon would feel sorry for him and she'd give in. Jenny knew all about it, and she didn't like him. She had known him before Sharon did, so she knew he had a mean and crazy side. She was afraid of him and those guys like him. She'd turn all of them away, and mostly they would stay in town.

Jenny was, Lily said, beyond emotions at this point. So much must have been going through her mind. She came back up to her cottage with the police and picked up a few things, including the gun, and then rode down to the station to give a statement.

"Don't you worry. I'll be back in a couple of hours," she told us. Then she left. The police said that if the coroner could determine that the gunshot didn't kill him she would only be charged with misconduct with a firearm, since she was defending herself.

Jenny walked down the path between the two policemen, looking small and out of her element. We sat down to a now cold stove and old coffee. The light of late morning was shining differently on the camp today. The fun and joviality of the previous day seemed like years in the past.

Chapter 20

The Town Visits

The police kept Jenny somewhat longer than expected, but by evening she came walking up the path, alone. She said they had removed Buck's body from the water and the county coroner was looking at it. They would tell her in a few days what she would be charged with.

Jenny sat at her kitchen table silently for a while. Then she started to talk about the police and how nice they were to her. Finally she started to cry, and she described the events of the previous evening. She had only meant to scare Buck. She had called him names, and said he was a bad man who had ruined her little family. He had shattered their easy way of life. She went on for a while, as Lily cooked and made coffee and tea for everyone and even pulled out the whiskey. Jenny went through the motions. She had coffee and then a little whiskey. When she went to bed Rachael went in and sat with her, but after a while Jenny shooed her out.

By morning things seemed to get back to normal. Jenny got up early and started cleaning. She cleaned and cleaned and then cleaned some more. She cleaned things that weren't even dirty. Then she went down to Sharon's and cleaned, bringing with her a little picture that she knew Sharon liked. They hung it in Sharon's kitchen. Sharon was in the cleaning spirit too, and she swept the path and the hill, cleaning away any sign of the previous night, even sweeping the bloody leaves down into the lake, where they drifted away. Both of them talked as they cleaned. They talked and talked and let the emotions run through them into the cleaning and talking frenzy.

Sharon was looking a little better. The swelling had gone down some and the bruising had colored up, but with the blood cleaned off she seemed to be closer to normal. Sharon was a big girl, which may account for why Buck was attracted to her, but it also helped her withstand some of the blows that might have ravaged a smaller woman.

By afternoon they were all up at Jenny's eating. Talk was of the last few days. While they tried to focus on the evening of the bed, it would inevitably go back to Buck. They were all working through it.

There hadn't been a visitor since the morning. We were settling in for coffee when we heard voices on the path. When Lily ducked outside we could hear her mutter a swear word. We all went out to the porch to see what was up.

A line of people trudged down the path, lots of townsfolk and church people. Lily could pick out a number of familiar faces. Jake and Betty were at the forefront. I couldn't believe my eyes. Surrounded by several others was Lucille, shrouded in black and wailing,

"You killed him!" Lucille pointed at Jenny. I could see the staging of a melodrama. "You killed my Buck! He was a good man and you are nothing but a two-bit whore up here, luring the good townsmen in like the sleazy, cheap white trash that you are." Lucille was just winding up, and murmurs of assent rose from the crowd. Several echoed "white trash."

"We want you out of town. The sheriff is gonna shut down this place, and all of you trash are going to have to leave, get out of town. Get it?" She went on, "And they should have taken that granddaughter of yours when they had the chance, before she turns out to be just like you."

That was a tack Lucille should have known better than to take. Jenny stepped forward from the group, her head up and chest out.

"Lu-cille Hunt," Jenny started. "You're going down the wrong avenue with me. You all high and mighty with that mean husband of yours. Why do you think he was up here? He was up here after that girl he got pregnant five years ago. Don't you remember the baby that was left at the convent? Who do you think the father was?"

A collective gasp and murmur came from the crowd. We all felt that Jenny might have gone too far, since Buck was barely cold.

"What are you saying?" Lucille was pale and more unsteady than when she started.

"You know damned well what I'm saying, you and all the rest of you coming up here. Jake, weren't you just here the other day? And you, Brian, didn't you just come up carrying a mattress for Lily with a couple of your buddies? And you, Deputy Hanson, I've seen you on this path. Don't you have a nerve to come up here like this! Half of you are cheaters, and the other half are hypocrites."

Jenny was on a roll, letting out all the resentment she'd been holding in for years. "I've spent my whole life feeling like I needed to atone for my sins, but I've come to realize that they are not my sins. They're yours. Yes, we do what we do here, and you may call it 'adultery,' and it may be a sin to you, but we couldn't do it without you." Jenny's voice stretched across the crowd, ringing out in a mighty crescendo that echoed across the ravine. "Yours are the sins of selfishness and discrimination, of intolerance and self-righteousness. Who's to judge which sins are greater?"

Those of us standing on the porch felt lifted up. We wanted to clap. It was all true, everything Jenny had said. We looked at her with pride, and then we watched as she leaned with her right arm against the porch post, then staggered, and then, in slow motion, fell into a heap on the ground.

Chapter 21

Jenny Goes to Town

Those of us on the porch ran over to her. She was pale and sweaty and panting. The townspeople were silent, watching. She was gasping for air and holding her chest. She started to turn a dark purple color. She looked in panic at Lily, who was holding her, cradling her. Jenny gasped several more times and then the breath in her went out in one last sigh. Lily held her as she went limp. She was dead.

The townspeople stood there. Several in the back were heard mumbling, "What are we doing here, anyway?"

Lily, still holding Jenny, spoke at last. "I think you've done enough. You've got what you came for."

The crowd broke up and turned back home. Even Lucille was silent, and with only one person at her elbow now, she went back down the path, followed by Jake and Betty.

We lifted Jenny up and carried her into her room. Lily and Rachael laid her out and sent me home, saying they needed to clean her up.

Rachael told me that after I left they washed her tired little frail body that just yesterday was so full of life. They dressed her in her favorite dress, the one with the flowers on it, and lit some candles. Lily and Rachael sat in there with her all night.

When I left, Emma and Linda and Sharon left with me and we all went into town. We knocked at the back door of the funeral director's home, and when he came they explained what they needed. I headed for home, my head swimming from the activities of these last few days. I was feeling punch-drunk, almost numb from emotion.

    Two mornings later I dressed up. I knew there would be a service for Jenny. On the way up to the camp I stopped at the mill and at several homes where I thought people would want to be involved. We all headed up there and saw the hearse backed up to the end of the dirt road, empty. At the camp several of the fellas were already milling around, looking sullen. When the undertaker emerged and asked for help, a bunch of them went in and came out carrying the simple casket where Jenny was resting. I went to help carry her up, and we all gently brought her to the pickup at the bottom of the dirt road that would take her to the hearse. A small parade followed us. We loaded her into the hearse and started through town. We went slowly, stopping in front of the church where another funeral, poorly attended, was taking place. The small crowd was swelling behind us. As we slowly wound our way through town we paused now and again, and people would come out to look, and some would follow. As we drew near the convent I recognized the tall black form of Sister Margaret, Bible in hand, patiently waiting for the procession. Once we were abreast of her she stepped out. The people nearby paused to let her join our solemn walk. We finally stopped at the mill. We took Jenny out where a table had been set up for us to have a ceremony, and placed the casket on some sawhorses draped in black crepe. It was lunch hour and a crowd of mill workers filed past her casket, touching it and shaking Lily's hand or embracing her. They shook Rachael's hand and the hand of each of the girls, solemnly offering their condolences. Sharon, still bruised, was the first to speak to the gathering circle.

    "Jenny was like a mother to me, and to all of us. She took us in and didn't ask questions. She was a good woman, maybe the best woman I've ever known. She didn't help just us, she helped all of you in one way or another." A murmur of assent went through the crowd. "What twist of fate puts us on the paths we lead? I don't have an answer for that. It's part of the mystery of life. I can only say that no matter what path we end up taking, the true person shines through. I only wish I could be as caring as Jenny was." Sharon was now in tears and moved back with the other girls. Lily embraced her.

A big black car drove up and in through the mill gate. A tall older man with silver hair, dressed nicely in a suit and tie, stepped out of the passenger side. He carried what looked like three dozen roses. He walked over to the casket and gently laid the roses on it. His head bowed and his hand reached out to the casket. He paused a few moments more, looked at Lily and nodded, then returned to the car. It drove away.

Harry came up from the back of the crowd, his long, slow stride certain and purposeful. Matilda was at his side, Sister Margaret left the crowd and moved to his other side. He stood behind the casket, opened the Bible in his hands, and began to speak.

"This Bible isn't mine. It's Jenny's. And even though she stopped going to church, she never lost faith. She said she didn't want to fluster the church folk – she was always thinking of other people." Then he started to read the Twenty-First Psalm.

"The Lord is my Shepherd, I shall not want…"

Everyone knew that Harry and Jenny were schoolmates, and some knew that she was sister to Margaret, but no one seemed to know who the mysterious stranger in the black car was. We followed the hearse up to the public cemetery on the hill where a grave had been dug, the dirt piled high on one side. The funeral director said a few words, and then invited everyone back to the French Club, where Lily had reserved some tables.

People filed into the club, and after the food had been served a keg was opened. What had started out sad and solemn began to become jovial. Everyone had a story or joke to tell about the camp or Jenny or the girls. The beer flowed, along with the tears and the laughter. Hot dogs were put on the griddle. It was the kind of sendoff that Jenny would have approved of.

Someone pulled out an accordion, then a fiddle appeared, and the dancing began and didn't end until they were locked out of the club at midnight. I danced with Rachael. We danced slowly, and every once in a while I was able to pull her close to me. I whispered in her ear those things we both knew, that she was the one for me, forever.

Jenny's Way

Part 2

Chapter 22

Camp Changes

Things changed at the camp. Lily moved into Jenny's cottage, taking her new bed with her. It barely fit, but she could not imagine leaving it. Sharon moved into Lily's. Emma and Linda were content as always in their cozy cottage. Now they were the first ones on the path and they got a few more customers. But even more important to them, they could monitor the comings and goings. No one was living at Sharon's. Sometimes Emma would bring her guests down there, and sometimes they would use it as a poker room or a place to sleep one off.

From time to time a regular left. Sometimes a younger man would get married and make an effort to be true to his wife. At times he might show up at the camp again after a marital tiff or just feeling the need to get away. Sometimes fellas just hang out, playing poker or drinking beer, talking or maybe even fishing, but they would still remember to bring up a little something. Once in a while a fella would want to simply run away when the pressure of the job or family life caught up with him. The girls would usually let him take Sharon's cottage until he was ready either to go back or to leave town for good. Like Jenny they did not accept anyone who was a troublemaker or law-breaker, but they were more likely than some of the townies to understand that there is more than one side to a story. There were a couple of guys who wanted to know more about how to please their wives, and the girls would take the time to show them how to patiently kiss and touch, and what felt good to women, and after a while these guys would stop coming to the camp.

Although business at the camp fell off for a time, the girls were never wanting for the necessities.

A mean little stone marked Buck's grave, and only once did flowers appear there.

A big stone was erected up at the cemetery where Jenny was buried, and on top was a sculptured granite urn with a cloth across the top. The engraving said she was a woman of generosity beyond her means. Every year on the anniversary of her birth a dozen roses showed up on her grave.

One afternoon Harry and I went fishing up towards the camp. After we caught a couple decent bass he suggested we share them with the girls. I had the impression he wanted to size up the camp and the girls still left there. I felt sure he didn't want to stop me from visiting, but wanted assurance I wouldn't be influenced to the bad. When we reached Jenny's old cottage Lily was at the stove, stoking it with small branches. She turned and smiled and beckoned us in.

"Sit down, Harry, John E. Take a load off," she said, pulling out the painted red chairs with the chipped decals and motioning towards them. Turning back to the stove she picked up the big black kettle and set it on one of the burners.

"Jenny thought the sun rose and set on you, John E., and she thought really highly of you and Matilda too, Harry."

"Strange how things work out, ain't it?" she continued. "She was thinking about getting out, leaving. She said someone asked her to go to a warmer climate. But she wasn't ready, didn't want to leave her family. That's how she thought of us, not just me and Rachael but the rest of the girls and some of the fellas too. She kept holding out, wanting to see Rachael get through high school, succeed, and get out of this life. Now she's gone, and who knows what will happen." Her voice started to sound thick, like she was struggling to maintain her composure. She poured some water into the teapot on the stove, jiggling the tea ball inside.

"How about some tea?" We both nodded our heads yes. "Things are changing around here. Oh, it might not be apparent yet, but there's a wind in the air. The mill's not doing as well as it did and a couple of the guys have been laid off. We'll probably be all right—

believe it or not Jenny was able to set aside a little nest egg for us and some of her friends helped out, so we should be okay for a while, but things are changing…" She trailed off.

While we were sitting there with Lily, sipping our tea, Sharon came in, smiling, almost bouncing. When she realized we were all at the table she turned quickly and pushed the guy who was following her out onto the porch, telling him to wait a second and she would be right out. She asked Lily for a couple of beers and when Lily nodded, went directly to the icebox and back out to the porch, giggling and murmuring to the fella as they walked down to her cottage.

"There's one right there. Sharon's got a regular fella – he's sweet on her and lately she's been seeing only him. God knows she deserves a happier life."

I hadn't seen Sharon since the funeral, when her face was still swollen and bruised and she looked mournful and downtrodden. I'd never before seen her quite as gleeful as I just had. Even in times of fun she always had an edge of sadness about her.

As we left and started off down the path, Harry seemed satisfied the camp hadn't changed for the bad. He didn't say a word, but I knew what that visit was about. For my part I was wondering where Rachael was and why she wasn't home. Sharon's cottage looked small and sad and deserted when we passed it. We looked at it and Harry voiced what we both were thinking: "I wonder what's going to become of this place and how long it will be before the town bucks up against them all again."

Chapter 23

The Flood

I remember that it started raining in mid-September. It rained for about four days.

Harry and Matilda had seen these bad storms and did their best to prepare for them. All the animals were secured with extra feed and water. Harry nailed wood across several of the windows in the house. We were fortunate to have just gotten the last of the hay and corn put up in the barn and silo. Harry had filled the fifty-gallon kerosene barrel and trimmed all the wicks of our lanterns. He thought we were ready, but he wasn't so sure that the rest of the town was.

The camp girls, who lived fairly simply, were able to move quickly. After the first day of rain almost none of the fellas were showing up at the camp. After the third day Sam went up and told the girls a hurricane was coming and they might want to go into town until it was over. The wind had started to blow and Lily thought they should get out. Each of them packed up what few valuables they had and put what they could as high up in the cottages as possible. Sharon and Lily packed everyone's linens into the washtubs, covered them with tarpaulin and put them into the back of Sam's pickup. Sam kindly drove down as close to the cottages as the muddy road would allow. Emma and Linda went to stay at the room of a fella they knew. Lily, Sharon and Rachael went to the convent, where Sister Margaret ushered them into one of the vacant rooms in the convalescent home. Lily and Rachael shared the single bed and Sharon slept on a cot Sister Margaret had brought in.

The wind was harsh and relentless. Branches and trees fell around the convent and church, and a portion of the road in front of the church was washed out. Lily and the girls were grateful for having the safety of brick and mortar, but also for being on the right side of the washout so they would be able to make their way back to their cottage homes. Word was coming in that dams upriver and downriver were washing out, but so far their strong Baltic dam was holding.

Once the storm subsided Emma and Linda found their way across the washout and told their terrible stories about the storm. They had been staying at a room on High Street. The raging winds and saturated ground had brought down dozens of the stately elms and maples that had arched over Main Street. The water had risen in the Big Flats area to almost the second floor of the homes there. They had to stay away from the windows for fear that a branch would get blown through the glass, but when the wind let up for a few minutes they would peek out at the devastation and watch, mesmerized, as sheds and boats floated through the village below. Floating trees and debris lodged against other trees and built up until those trees holding the mass gave way and all was swept away.

The homes on Little Flats were half submerged and the water was running wildly around the Men's Club and the boardinghouse, both of which looked badly damaged. The telephone poles were down but the town had lost electricity a day earlier. The girls said that nothing looked as it once had, but our dam held. The water came over the dam like Niagara Falls, a great roar that could be heard all over the little valley. All the women worried about their cottages.

For the next two days they all stayed at the convalescent home. Gradually the water started to recede from the village, and the clean-up work started. Sam picked them up and drove as far as he could down the dirt road to Jenny's Way until a washout stopped him. They all walked the rest of the way, and were shocked at the devastation. Two large trees had fallen into the road. To make it passable they would have to be removed and the road at the washouts repaired. When they got to the cottages they saw water still up to the porches, lapping at the porch decking. Debris was everywhere. Sharon's old cottage, the closest to the water, got the worst of the damage. The door was open and water had washed away some of the meager furniture and disturbed the rest, moving the table, knocking chairs over and soaking the bed mattress. They all gathered shovels, brooms, mops and rags and helped sweep out the mud and layers of leaves. Lily's cottage had a broken window pane that we temporarily boarded over; luckily it was under the porch roof and wouldn't get much rain. It looked like all the other cottages had at one point been flooded up to an inch or so. Dirt and mud and piles of leaves had been dumped into corners of the porches, where the receding waters trapped them. A couple of barrels that had been on the porch were lost. The dock was gone and a sad little rowboat that was always pulled up onto the shore had also disappeared. But they had been spared the worst of the storm.

Lily and the girls cleaned up their cottages. Sam brought in a couple of guys with two-person crosscut saws to cut up the trees blocking the road so they could be pushed out of the way. Once the girls were comfortable again they went into town to help with the cleanup there. Everyone got typhoid shots. While the fire department pumped water out of the cellars of the duplexes, they swept and mopped and even helped to cut up some trees. Sharon put on a pair of men's pants someone loaned her and a pair of leather work gloves and worked one half of a two-man saw. They all raked and dragged branches and scooped buckets of mud from the cellars. They piled up masses of broken furniture and wood that had been washed down, then loaded it all onto trucks that hauled it out of town. A tent was erected for people working on the cleanup and food and drink was provided. There was a rare sense of camaraderie that the girls seldom felt with the townies. But once the cleanup was over they could feel the climate changing. They were the target of little comments and the cold shoulders of many of the women, and even some of the men they knew. Feeling shunned again, they went back to their simple lives at the cottages.

Chapter 24

Lucille 'nd Kevin

I never liked Buck. He seemed like a mean and unpredictable man. Yet for all the mistrust I had, I still felt bad for Lucille and even for Kevin. Word went around at school about the father's hardness and how sad their family life was. Sometimes, before Buck died, Kevin would show up at school with bruises, but he brushed them off by claiming to have had a fight with a high school kid in which he was the victor. Neighbors would talk. Guys who came up to the camp would talk. After Buck died it was a regular topic of conversation, at the coffee shop, at the barbershop, around kitchen tables. A picture of the family emerged and as a town we watched its tortured history unfold.

Lucille, for all her shock and anger over discovering the alliance between Sharon and Buck, was truly pained by Buck's loss. He was cruel and abusive, but she had learned to deflect his anger when he was drunk. She remembered their first meetings and how gallant he could be when some of the guys in town mocked her for being on the pudgy side. He'd take a poke at them and they would apologize, because they knew that if he was seriously angry with them they had little chance of coming out victorious. He would protect her, then turn around and swing at her himself. She became very sensitive to his moods and knew the instant he stepped through the door whether he'd been drinking or not. If he had had a good day they might have a nice dinner and some fun, or occasionally he'd take her out to the diner for dinner or try to talk her into accompanying him to the bar. Before she realized he had a drinking problem they would go out to the bar together and enjoy some of the evening. He might even get frisky and pull her up for a dance or two. But as he kept drinking he became more and more surly and rough, and then you had to be careful what you said and how you said it. She tried to avoid him when he drank at the house because she didn't want to have the neighbors in the other side of the duplex hear him shout and throw things around.

But he was a good provider and the good times just about outweighed the bad, so she stayed. Besides, who else would have her?

Kevin, big and brutish and angry, was following in his father's footsteps. Buck had taken his anger out on Kevin too, cussing him out in public and telling him he was stupid and never going to make anything of himself. Occasionally Buck treated him well; he'd take him out to the pharmacy, where they'd sit on the stools and have ice cream sundaes and soda. Kevin adored him, looking for his praise like a puppy to his master, but praise wasn't often lavished on him. Usually it was the back of Buck's hand or a curse that was thrown his way. He took to bullying his classmates and Buck encouraged this – told him he was pleased he could hold his own, told him not to let anyone get the better of him. Buck honed Kevin's aggression like a knife, saying he was proud of his playground bullying and then turning around and swatting him for not running quickly enough to get him a beer. Kevin was yearning for the love and caring his father couldn't give him. Buck knew he should reach out to Kevin, but he couldn't. He saw too much of himself and his own father in the boy—the cruel and brutish reaction to too little love—and he loathed the similarities. Love frightened Buck. It meant you were weak and vulnerable, and he wouldn't have any of it, and wouldn't have his kid all needy either. This tug of push and pull nearly drove Kevin insane. One minute he'd be on top of the world, the next he was miserable. Lucille could see it all, but she couldn't give Kevin what he needed. What else could Kevin do but meet any praise or love from her with disdain? She thought he didn't respect her because Buck didn't. This was the painful triangle of emotions that was broken with Buck's death. Could Kevin be saved from a life at the bar, brawling like his father? Maybe Lucille could have done it, but she did something totally unexpected.

Chapter 25

Lucille's Discovery

Lucille had one friend in the world, one person she trusted, and that was Betty. She and Betty had been united by their disgust with the camp girls, the "damned hussies up the lake." Lucille would stop and talk to Betty every time she went by the butcher shop and sometimes they'd go next door and have a coffee at the pharmacy counter, stewing over their desire to eliminate the camp. What Lucille didn't know was that Betty didn't think that much of her. Other than their joint dislike Betty thought they didn't have much in common. In fact, Betty saw Lucille as beneath her. So Betty talked. She felt she had to share what she heard and she shared it with Jake. But Betty was wily enough to know what to reveal and what to hold back. After all, no plan to rid the town of whores would work if she shared it with someone known to visit them. So she told Jake only about Lucille's plans for the future and her problems with Kevin and, to influence him, how the camp had ruined a perfectly good marriage.

Jake was the butcher, and a well-liked guy. People would come into the shop and swap jokes and news all day long. What was the point, Jake thought, of people shopping there if you couldn't offer services that the big markets didn't have time for? So Jake joked, and talked, and gossiped. He would still sneak up to the camp too, when he could get away undetected, and he talked some more. So we heard all the news, including what Betty was up to. I was almost embarrassed to get such personal details, but, like being drawn to a train wreck, I couldn't turn completely away.

Lucille, in her pain over losing Buck, did what she thought would help, trying to bring Buck back in some way, back into her life, and maybe Kevin's too. Or, we speculated, maybe it was just her attempt to feel whole and happy for once. After a few months she found herself walking by the fenced playground near the convent, the playground where the kids who were wards of the state played, the kids that the Sisters cared for. She'd search the yard for boys about four or five years old, boys she might recognize. Finally, one cloudy day a boy in a jacket that looked too small for him on the playground with another boy. He had an awkward look about him, a look of someone grown too big too fast. But he also had another look, a sweet, innocent and kind look, which drew her to him like a magnet. She passed by the playground more and more often and when she saw him she watched him, shyly at first. But then she couldn't help but just stand and stare, holding onto the wrought-iron fence, smiling, smiling at the blond curly-haired boy. He would see her and watch her too. Sometimes she'd smile and he'd smile back. After a few weeks he would look for her standing by the fence, and wave when he got on the swing, and wave again when the nuns called him back in. Finally one day he approached Lucille at the fence.

"Hi. My name is Michael. The nuns call me Michael like the angel. They say I'm an angel sent from Heaven, 'cause an angel left me on their doorstep."

He smiled the smile of a cherub, melting Lucille's heart. He was beautiful, not dark like Buck or Kevin and without the heavy brow. She wanted to hug him, to hold him, to make him safe and happy. But she only shook his hand through the fence and said, "Hi. My name is Lucille."

The next day she went to the convent and started adoption proceedings.

This was not an easy process. The nuns had grown attached to Michael, and if they were going to be required to give him up they wanted to be sure it was to a good home. The nuns and the priest asked her all kinds of personal questions. Lucille no longer had a husband, and although Buck had left her some money, would it be enough to provide for two children and herself? She would get a job. Would it be a healthy house without a father? It would be a loving but small family, and his uncle could spend time with him. Would the taint of a drunken father mark the son? The priest and sisters were not going to give him up easily, even when Lucille got a lawyer to resist their efforts to keep him. It cost more money than she could easily afford. Even the lawyer advised against it, but in the end she prevailed, and after a battle that dragged on for months, Michael went home with Lucille. The nuns gathered and some tears were shed, but Lucille in her daily visits to Michael finally convinced the nuns and Michael that she would provide a happy home for him. He came down the steps with his little cardboard suitcase, his teddy bear under his arm. The nuns gave him a paper sack with more clothes and a missal and a little St. Michael medal that they hung around his neck. He cried, but Lucille plied him with an offer of an ice cream soda at the diner on the way home and talked about his new bedroom he would have all to himself, and of his new brother, Kevin.

  Lucille imagined a new life, a happy life, giving this child the family that he never had. Taking this child that was Buck's would help to atone somehow for all the ills that Buck had brought on them both. Lucille would save Michael, and Michael would save the family. Lost in her grief, Lucille's vision was blurred by her desire for a happier life. The clarity of hindsight sometimes comes too late.

Chapter 26

A Newcomer

We heard snippets of all this from the duplex neighbor and from the counter girl at the pharmacy where they stopped for ice cream sodas. Sipping them, they talked about the new home and bedroom that Michael would be moving into. They talked about the old school Michael would continue to attend, still able to see his caretakers the nuns, still able to see his friends. She asked him if he like to play sports, and which ones. She asked if he liked school and what classes he liked, and if he could read, and what books he liked. She told him they were going to buy their duplex, which for the first time the mills were offering to sell. Some people had already purchased them and added on a porch or repainted with a color other than the mill's standard white.

On the way home from the diner they stopped at the general store, where Lucille intended to pick up a few groceries. There she saw a new baseball glove and baseball, the leather stitching clean and the smooth palm uncreased. Suddenly she felt she wasn't adequate. After all her battling to get him, what if he wasn't happy with them? She felt she needed to give Michael something, something to help make him like her and the new home. She purchased the baseball glove and ball.

When they arrived home Lucille showed Michael around: kitchen, living room, backyard, new bedroom. Together they put his small pile of clothes into his dresser, his little comb on the top, and then his toothbrush in the bathroom. When they went back to his room Lucille brought out the new baseball glove and ball.

"Michael, we're so happy to have you come live with us, to be in our family. Here is a present for you, something you can use when you go out and play with the kids at school." She took the glove and ball out of the bag and laid them on the bed.

"This is for me?" he said, looking at the glove and then at her. He walked over and hugged her. Lucille's heart almost burst. "Yes, honey, for you."

He went back to the bed, picked up the glove with both hands and tried to put his hand into it. The glove was ridiculously large for him. As he wriggled his fingers into the finger holes, trying to make it fit, Kevin stepped from the doorway into the room, grabbed the glove from Michael's hand, threw it onto the floor and stomped on it, screaming, "You stupid bitch! You never gave me a glove! You never gave me a ball! Don't I deserve it? Don't I deserve as good as this little shit?"

He shoved Michael back onto the bed and ran from the room, sobbing and screaming obscenities until they could hear the door slam behind him.

Michael started to cry. Lucille stood there, stunned. She could already see more than hairline cracks in her perfect little picture. How silly to imagine she could have a happy home, a good life. How foolish. She calmly walked over to Michael and hugged him, holding him with one arm against her and picking up the glove with the other hand.

"He didn't mean that," she said in a soothing tone. "He just misses his daddy." She handed the glove back to Michael, brushing it off on her dress, but he pushed it away and would have none of it.

And so began Michael's new life with Lucille and Kevin.

Michael, the sensitive, sweet and bright angel. Kevin, the brutish angry lout. Over and over again the scene was repeated. Kevin never embraced the role of older brother, seeing the interloper only as someone he could never outshine in his mother's eyes, but someone his father would have viewed as a sissy. It was his only solace, believing that his father would have chosen him over the fair-haired boy. Michael was a wimp, he thought, who never would have survived the rough treatment Buck meted out to Kevin.

Michael became more sensitive. Fears bloomed where only childhood simplicity once existed. Lucille fretted and tried to mediate, but Kevin would lean around her from both sides, hurling epithets at Michael, who withdrew more and more.

Lucille would go to Betty, asking her advice. After all, Betty had a boy who wasn't a model child. What could she do? Betty just shook her head and offered "tsk, tsk, tsk."

Chapter 27

A Bad Turn

Now and then Sister Margaret would meet Lily and they would share whatever news there was. Generally Sister Margaret wouldn't spread what she considered gossip, but she was concerned about Michael and wanted to know what Lily had heard about Lucille. The nuns had begun to see changes in Michael, see him become quieter, smiling less, and becoming agitated as the school day came to a close. They noticed his reluctance to meet Lucille at the gate for the walk home. These and other little signs made them ask Lucille if there was a problem at home. Lucille, unable to admit to the troubles they were having, still faithful to Buck and Kevin, denied any issues, blaming it all on his difficulty with some of the classes at school.

Lily told Sister Margaret what she'd heard but she didn't know the full measure of the problem and told her to talk to Betty, who might have more information.

Betty was excited to have a visit from Sister Margaret, who had never called on her before. She asked her in for tea and biscuits. Sister Margaret gingerly worked around to the subject of Lucille and Michael. Normally Betty might have been suspicious, but this was Sister Margaret. She felt she was privileged to be held in the Sisters' confidence. She told her what she knew.

The pieces started to come together. Michael seemed happy when he was home alone with Lucille, while Kevin was out with his pals tormenting other kids or animals, but as evening drew near he became more and more alarmed. She often sent him to bed early just to avoid the face-offs that happened on such a regular basis. But recently she had also noticed Kevin wouldn't get home until 9 or 10 at night. If she was still up ironing or cleaning, he'd brush by her on the way to the kitchen for something to eat or drink and he'd smell like smoke and sometimes like alcohol. She'd tried to talk to him. "Kevin, honey, is everything all right? Do you want me to make some of that fried chicken you like so much? I could have it for you tomorrow, ready when you get out of school."

"Just mind your own business, Ma." Kevin's tone was surly. "I don't know when I'll be getting home tomorrow," he said over his shoulder on his way up the stairs with a glass of milk and a handful of cookies.

Lucille didn't know what to do. He was taller now than she was, with his father's rough strength. While he'd never raised a hand to her, the underlying tension and feeling that violence was just under the surface kept her from pushing any further. What good would it do anyway? She couldn't control him. She didn't know what he was doing and tried not to think too much about it.

One night around 11 o'clock, while Lucille was dozing in a living room chair, there was a knock on the door. She awoke with a snort and sat upright. She knew what it was. She had known this day would come even though she never admitted it to herself. The knock came again, louder. She rose, straightened her hair, and answered the door. A police officer stood there with his arm through Kevin's.

"Are you Mrs. Hunt?" Lucille nodded yes.

"Is this your son, Mrs. Hunt?"

Lucille nodded again, staring at Kevin, his face red and sweaty and swollen. The officer helped Kevin into the house and backed him towards a chair. Kevin put his hand back to be sure he could find the chair behind him as he sat down.

"Well, Mrs. Hunt, your son here has gotten himself into some trouble. He and a couple of his pals were down at the corner liquor store trying to steal a bottle of whiskey. One of them created a diversion while the other slipped a flat bottle up his sleeve. Well, I guess it wasn't the first time, so Mr. Bartholomew was able to catch them this time. He grabbed Kevin, but his buddy got away. Kevin gave him a couple of punches, but Bart was a little bigger and was able to tackle him. Now Bart is a good guy, and knew Buck, and feels bad about your family situation, so he's not pressing charges, but you'd better get this fellow under control before he gets into serious trouble."

Lucille was crushed. Not only was it a public humiliation that would be all over town since it was likely her neighbor in the duplex was listening. Not only would it jeopardize her adoption of Michael, since the State workers were still visiting. But she also knew in her heart there was no way she could control Kevin. Could she say that to the police? Could she just say to them, Take him away, straighten him out, I can't? No, she couldn't say it. She couldn't admit she'd failed him, that she couldn't raise them both, that she wasn't strong enough.

She just nodded her head yes. "Thank you, officer. Thank you for bringing him home."

Kevin, sitting at an awkward, drunken angle, laughed, and mimicked Lucille, "Yeah, thanks, officer," and laughed again.

The policeman looked at him and knew. Lucille didn't have to tell him she couldn't control him. She didn't have to tell him anything. He knew it all. He'd seen it all before. Some people couldn't be reached, couldn't be changed, and couldn't change themselves. He turned around and walked down the steps, shaking his head. "Goodnight, Mrs. Hunt." She watched him leave, all hope lost. With a deep sigh she shut the door and walked upstairs, not even looking at Kevin, not even trying to discipline him.

"Goddammit!" Kevin screamed at her back as she went up the stairs. "Goddammit! Aren't you going to even holler at me? Aren't you gonna even try?" He picked up an ashtray and hurled it up the stairs after her, but she just closed her door on him as he started to sob.

Policemen visited the camp, so we heard all the news.

Kevin was gone in the morning when Lucille got up. She found out later he had been skipping school and hanging out by the diner or down by the tracks where the vagrants hung out, bumming cigarettes from them and swapping tales of grandiose adventures.

Once in a while he'd steal a few dollars from the pension that Buck left and get one of the bums to buy him a pint.

He thought about getting a job at the mill. They wouldn't hire him full time until he was old enough, but he might be able to get enough money to rent a room somewhere. He didn't think he was that bad. He just needed a chance. But toeing the line seemed almost impossible. People wanted the impossible. Maybe he could find a girlfriend, someone to love him, and they could get an apartment. He just needed a chance. He told Sarge his problems, standing at the corner loitering, told him how nobody understood him. Told him how Lucille replaced him with a little piss-ant and how Buck wouldn't have liked the little sweet face and would have straightened that kid out. He imagined that Lucille hated him, and he despised her. She was his mother, dammit! Why didn't she love him?

Sarge thought that deep down he just needed more love than she could give, maybe more than anyone could. He listened to it all and just agreed quietly, knowing he couldn't argue. Besides, maybe he'd get a few cigarettes out of it. But later he'd tell the bartender, and the bartender would tell Jake, and Jake would tell Lily.

Kevin poured his heart out never knowing that half the town's tongues were wagging. All these things he shared, imagining the best of the possibilities. Never imagining the worst.

Chapter 28

Rachael and Lily

One afternoon when I visited, Rachael was down at the river and Lily had me sit at the table with her. She talked about what she thought was going on with Rachael and asked me questions about it. Rachael talked to me too, and so I had pieced together a picture of the camp now that Jenny was gone. Rachael missed Jenny more than anyone else did. Jenny was like a mother to her, a warm, nurturing, wise mother. It didn't seem possible to her that Jenny would just die like that, here one minute, calling out the names of the townies, and gone the next. How could it happen? She didn't even get to say goodbye to her. She couldn't understand the finality of it, couldn't get her mind around it. She would lie in bed in the morning listening to Lily stoke the stove and think it was Jenny. And then she'd remember, and put her face in her pillow and cry. She'd come out of her bedroom all red-faced and Lily would hold her and stroke her hair and try to comfort her. But there was no comfort for this ache, no salve for this wound. Lily knew it would just take time, but Rachael didn't understand about time, when even a year still seemed like eternity to her.

Rachael grew moody and sullen, so unlike the quiet, sweet girl that Lily knew. At times she withdrew and would spend hours alone by the lake reading. She would ask if anyone needed something in town and if Sharon or Emma did she would walk down and back, often several times a day. Once in a while she would snap at Lily and then quickly apologize. Lily realized she missed Jenny and tried to be gentle, but she also realized that Rachael was going through some growing pains and had very few other kids her age to spend time with.

Whenever I saw Lily she confided in me more and more. I didn't have the answers she was looking for and suggested she visit Sister Margaret. The light came into her eyes. She said I was right and made me feel like some kind of prophet. So, after weeks of trying to figure out what to do, Lily visited Sister Margaret. She needed to understand, she needed to get some help. Sister Margaret heard Lily out, alternately nodding and shaking her head. Then she suggested that Rachael get involved with some after-school activities, maybe spend more time away from home. Maybe help tutor some of the younger kids in reading, maybe join the chorus – things that would widen her circle of acquaintances. Lily had always wanted to keep Rachael close, thinking she was protecting her, but she was seeing that it might be time to let her go a little, to let her learn more about the larger world. Rachael did go to school in town, but once the school day was over she would came straight home, only making short visits to the corner general store. Between them they planned out how they would best present it to her. Sister Margaret would mention that she needed help tutoring the younger children, and Lily would approach Rachael that evening. I was there when she did.

"Hi, Bunny," she said when Rachael came in that afternoon. Rachael changed her clothes and came with her books to the kitchen table, getting ready to do her homework by the fading window light.

"I was in town today talking to Sister Margaret," Lily began. Rachael looked up from her notebook.

"She said she was looking for help tutoring and I said you might want to help out…"

Rachael looked at her and smiled, then put down her pencil and got up and hugged Lily. "Thanks, Ma," she said. "I would really like to do that." Lily thought her heart would break. In this bittersweet moment she realized her girl was growing up.

And that was how Rachael's transition to the other world began.

Chapter 29

The New World

I would pass the classroom where Rachael was tutoring after school. In truth I wanted to be the one she was tutoring. In Rachael Sister Margaret and the other nuns found a helpful, pleasant tutor. Everyone began to rely more and more on her, and they found she was quite capable and responsible. Once when I went by her classroom and peeked in Sister Margaret came up next to me and watched also. She shook her head. "A girl coming from the cottages—who would have thought she would become such a fine lady?" Then, looking at me, she appeared suddenly embarrassed. "You understand what I mean, John E." I nodded. I seemed to have become everyone's confidant.

Rachael blossomed. She became so popular among the children that the nuns had to decide carefully which ones she would tutor each week, and they sometimes found that children who did not even require help were applying. Sister Margaret would pass by a classroom and see Rachael's head bent next to a little red-headed boy, who was beaming up at her. She watched, listening to Rachael's murmurs of encouragement and her light laughter when the little student suddenly understood.

Rachael told me Sister Margaret asked if she would be interested in joining the school choir. She had heard her sing in music class and thought her clear, rich voice would be an asset to the choir and offer Rachael another avenue to become more involved with the school and the convent. Rachael was afraid Lily wouldn't let her join. It meant more time away, and sometimes bus trips to other towns for choral meets and concerts. As it was, Rachael was spending more and more time at the school. Lily reluctantly agreed, knowing that saying no was not really an option, but she sent a note to Sister Margaret via Rachael, asking her to please have someone accompany Rachael home if she was attending a late concert. And I offered to do that whenever I was available.

Rachael became the anchor of the choir, and while she was too shy to sing solos, hers was the clear strong voice that all the others seemed to follow. She made friends, and although she was never in the most elite cliques, she was popular and sought after at lunch and at informal socials. Lily did her best to see that her clothes were not old-fashioned; while simple and sturdy, they had an almost classic look.

I could see that Rachael's life had changed; although she still missed Jenny she didn't notice it as much when she was at school. But she told me the dull ache would come back when she walked the path home in the evening.

A concert was coming up that required a very late bus. Concerned for her safety, Sister Margaret got Lily's permission for Rachael to stay at the convent that night. So that evening, after the concert, Rachael stayed in one of the tiny spare rooms that the nuns slept in. With only a bed, chair, night table and hooks on the wall, it did not feel overly different from her bedroom, except perhaps for the crucifix over the bed. She was enjoying this new world, a world of indoor toilets and electric lights. In the morning she luxuriated in the steaming bath in the large enamel tub – a very rare extravagance for her. The camp was feeling more and more foreign to her, and less and less desirable. Yet Lily was there, keeping her room ready and making her breakfasts and dinners, smiling when she walked in with her pile of books.

I walked Rachael home when I could, but often I had to be at the farm and she walked home alone. She said these lone walks through the village in the evening were pleasant and quiet, giving her time to reflect on the day and to plan for the next day. She would usually see people she knew, many of them men who visited the camp somewhat regularly or once had. They all knew her and all had a warm and protective attitude towards her. She'd pass by a group of fellas smoking outside a bar and speak to them, knowing many by name. They always smiled and tipped their hats and would tell her to give their regards to one girl or another. She felt safe. But there was one person who would have made her nervous on her way home. Fortunately, she never met him.

Chapter 30

The Gift

A spring dance was to be held at the school auditorium. I invited Rachael to go with me and she excitedly accepted. She had planned to wear one of her school dresses but Lily wanted her to look and feel special, so she had one of the girls get a new dress, a simple light blue cotton one with white lace at the top of the bodice, gathered at the waist with a sash. Lily let down the hem a little and spent extra time starching and ironing it, grateful that Rachael was not overly clothes-conscious. On the evening of the dance Rachael donned a favorite school dress and came into the kitchen. On the table was a package wrapped in brown paper and string.

"Why don't you open this? You may be able to use it tonight." Lily carelessly pushed the package towards her. Rachael stood staring at it, not fully understanding that it was for her and a surprise. When she opened it and held it up, tears welled in her eyes and Lily's too.

"Oh Ma, it's beautiful!" She swung it around and caressed the lace.

"Hurry up. Get in there and try it on. You don't want to be too late." Lily pushed her towards her room.

Rachael came out looking like a princess, like a woman. Lily was so proud of this beautiful young lady. Rachael twirled around for Lily to see the fit and fall of the dress. It *was* perfect, the right size, the right length, the right color to set off her dark brown hair held back with a matching blue ribbon.

They sat down together for a cup of tea. Rachael waited nervously; fearful she might spill tea but too excited to stay still long.

Lily brought out her shears and a towel and trimmed Rachael's hair so that it lay evenly across the back of the dress.

That was when I arrived. Lily was shaking the towel into the leaves off the porch. I sat down for a few minutes to have some tea and hear the story of the new dress. Lily and Rachael chattered together, barely taking a breath. I hadn't been visiting as often as I had been so Lily was full of news and Rachael was nervously filling in any details she'd miss. Farming had been taking up more of my time and school had taken up more of Rachael's. When we got up to go and I carefully pinned a small corsage onto Rachael's dress, I caught Lily wiping her eyes and watching us as I took Rachael's hand to usher her down the path. The strong attachment we had formed was growing steadily.

From her porch Lily watched us walk down the path together, the warm spring air fresh and rich. Sometimes Rachael sought out my hand to help her over a small rivulet. Lily watched until we were out of view. We could dimly hear boaters on the lake, a few evening birds, and a woman's laughter somewhere out of sight.

Lily said Rachael and I made a handsome couple, both of us tall and slender and attractive. I wore one of my best white shirts, neatly pressed black trousers and my best shoes. Nervous with excitement we entered the auditorium, going first to say hello to Sister Margaret, who was chaperoning, then to the table of punch and cookies, then to a couple of the metal chairs that were set up around the dance floor. We tried to look grown-up and comfortable. Shortly some of our friends came over and sat with us and we all talked with an unusual attempt at maturity, until Gerry Murphy made a joke about one of the guys and everyone loosened up.

Rachael and I danced waltzes, close, but not so close that Sister Margaret would have to come over and remind us of the rules of conduct on the dance floor. This would occasionally happen to some of the couples, and once a couple was even thrown out for refusing to maintain a "decent" distance while close-dancing. One of the guys brought a half pint of brandy and passed it around in the boy's lavatory to anyone who was brave enough to drink it. I wasn't.

The time flew, and before I knew it the lights flickered the signal for the last dance.

Rachael had planned to stay overnight at the convent after the dance so she could help Sister Margaret and the other nuns clean up the auditorium. We danced the last slow dance and I was able to draw her closer and take deep breaths into her hair, wanting to inhale all her wonderful scent. Rachael saw me to the door of the auditorium and we kissed lightly on the lips, waving at each other as I started my walk home.

Rachael began her task, picking up paper cups and napkins and wiping up spilled punch. Then she collected a few of the last dangling streamers as some of the boys put away the folding chairs. She swept the stage while the boys swept the auditorium.

All the leftover cups and napkins and punchbowls were piled at the door to go back to the school kitchen. Amongst them was a beautiful bouquet of spring daffodils. Seeing them, Rachael realized with a start that tomorrow would be Lily's birthday, and daffodils were her favorite flower. She had been so caught up in her own excitement that she had forgotten her mother's birthday. She wanted to ask for the bouquet and bring it home for Lily that night. She thought she might have to lie to Sister Margaret, telling her that I was waiting to walk her home; otherwise they would insist she stay the night. But she hated to lie, and hoped she could slip out without being noticed. She didn't want to have to trouble anyone to walk her up to the back path into the woods. That would be too embarrassing.

Chapter 31

The Bouquet

Rachael was able to sneak out undetected with her bouquet for Lily. The moon was full so she knew she would have no trouble negotiating the path home.

By this time it was very late. Bars were letting out and drunks were making their way home or gathered in little groups, smoking, talking and laughing, sometimes passing around a bottle someone had clipped. She walked briskly past them. Occasionally someone who recognized her would say goodnight. When she got close to the edge of town she saw someone in the streetlight's shadow, leaning against the façade of the butcher shop, smoking. It was Kevin. She decided it was too late to cross the street, for surely he had seen her and it might provoke him. She thought if she just kept walking, not slowing down, pretending not to notice him, he might not bother her. As she passed him she could hear him shout, "Hey! Are you too good to say goodnight to me? Hey, you, Rachael, I'm talking to YOU."

His voice got louder when she kept right on walking and didn't reply. She heard him start to follow her, and when they got alongside the alley to the butcher's shop back door, he grabbed her arm and pulled her into the alley so quickly she had no time to respond. In a second he was behind her and had her head in a headlock. A knife came from nowhere and he held it in front of her face with his free arm and in a gritty whisper next to her head he threatened, "You scream and I'll cut your throat."

He threw her onto the ground, straddled her and ripped the bodice of her new dress open, tearing the lace and her slip and bra beneath, all the while holding the knife in his other hand.

"You dumb bitch. You think you're so hoity, but you're just the whore's daughter. Well, here's what we do to whores' daughters."

He pulled up her dress. Ripping her underwear, he forced her legs apart with his.

Rachael didn't have a chance. As tall as she was, he was taller and broader and drunk. She started to fight with her arms but he hit her across the mouth so hard she stopped struggling, dazed and bleeding. He raped her.

Before he staggered out of the alley he hit her again and left her lying unconscious, the bouquet of daffodils strewn about her.

He picked up the bottle he had left by the front of the butcher shop and took another swig, then stumbled home.

Lucille heard him come in, but decided she would talk to him in the morning.

Chapter 32

Lost

Rachael came to, not knowing where she was, feeling dazed, in pain, and lost. Then all that had transpired just minutes before came back to her. She sat up, looked at the mangled daffodils strewn about her in disarray, and started to cry. But fearing that Kevin might return, she stifled her tears and stood up, trying to straighten her dress and pull up the torn bodice. Between small choking sobs, she picked up the crushed daffodils and hobbled back to the sidewalk. She walked, as quickly as her bruised body allowed, towards the road to Lily's. As she went by Beaver Brook she threw the daffodils into it, her gaze following them as they were caught in a lazy eddy and disappeared into the dark waves. She turned down the road and then limped stiffly up the path.

She stole quietly past all the cottages and slipped silently into her bedroom, not wanting to see Lily, not wanting to see anyone. She was ashamed. Embarrassed, ashamed and in pain. What had she done? Why had she let herself be used by that wretched boy? She could no longer be a tutor at the school. She would no longer be the darling of the nuns. She was a marked woman. She had avoided Sister Margaret and slipped out, and now she had paid for that deviousness with her honor. She was doomed to be a camp girl like her mother and grandmother. Even less than a camp girl. She hated it, she hated Kevin, and she hated herself. John E. wouldn't want her. No one would. She would be the laughingstock of the school. School? She couldn't even go back to school. She couldn't tell anyone. But could she keep it a secret? She was hurt. She was dirty. She was torn.

She took the dress off, held it up, and wept softly. Maybe she could mend it. She lit a candle and crept out into the kitchen to dampen a facecloth with hot water from the stove reservoir, then slipped back into her room. She looked in the mirror and started to wash her face. It was a different face. It was older, more serious, cut and bruised, and frowning back at her. She gently washed tender spots on her shoulders and then on her legs, wiping away blood and fluids and dirt. She went back and got a little more hot water and once again washed herself. Then she took two aspirin and lay awake until almost dawn, thinking up elaborate stories to explain to Lily her bruises and torn dress.

Years later she told me about that night, about the pain, the anguish, and how ashamed she felt.

Chapter 33

The Family

No one was at Lucille's the next morning, the morning after Rachael was raped. No one could tell us exactly what happened. This is what we pieced together from the neighbors and the gossips.

As Lucille started downstairs to make coffee and breakfast she paused to push open Kevin's door, which was partially closed. Kevin lay on the bed in his clothes. He'd fallen asleep just where he fell the night before, not only disheveled but dirty and with blood on his clothes, scratches on his face, and what looked like a half pint of brandy near his open hand.

She stood there, just watching him deep in a heavy-breathing sleep. How did it come to this? Buck could have at least kept a tighter rein on him. He'd had the size to intimidate. She felt powerless. But she couldn't take it anymore. She had to do something to straighten him out.

She went down to the kitchen and started coffee. She took out eight eggs and a pound of bacon, separated the bacon in a cast iron frying pan, and lit the fire under it. She broke the eggs into a bowl, added milk and pepper and salt and scrambled them all together, then put them aside and waited for the bacon to finish. As it crisped up she pulled it off piece by piece, laying it to drain on an old paper bag. She poured off a little of the bacon grease into a coffee can, then emptied the eggs into the pan. Taking out the bread, she put two pieces into the toaster, readying it. The butter was already on the table in the butter dish, soft and sweet. When the eggs were half done she took the pan off the heat, covered it, and went upstairs to wake Kevin.

"Kevin, Kevin, come on down and have some breakfast. I cooked up some nice bacon and eggs and coffee and it's all ready." Her tone was slightly pleading. Kevin stirred a little and Lucille prodded him, pushing on the arm he was holding over his eyes to block the light. A knife fell out of his hand onto the bed next to him.

"What in the hell? Kevin! GET UP! KEVIN!" Kevin woke. He sat up on the side of the bed, covering his eyes with one hand, moaning slightly.

"WHAT – IS – GOING ON?" Lucille was starting to lose control.

"Get out of here and leave me alone, dammit." He was still sitting with his head in one hand, leaning on the bed with the other. But she just stood there, hands on her hips, disapproving.

In a flash he was on her, knocking her to the floor, straddling her, his hands around her neck. She had only a moment to shriek before he tightened his hold and shook and shook as her face got redder and her eyes bulged out and her arms flailed trying to pull his arms away, but he held on until she stopped struggling, and then stopped moving altogether.

"There, you dumb bitch, THAT'S what's going on." He got off her and went into the bathroom to pee.

Michael woke from all the commotion and came to the door, rubbing his eyes. He stared open-mouthed at Lucille on the floor, and then looked at Kevin emerging from the bathroom, buttoning his fly. He was paralyzed, but in the split second it took for him to understand and turn to run, Kevin was on him too.

Grabbing Michael by the arm, Kevin hit him so viciously that Michael never felt the next blows that crushed his skull when it was slammed against the floor. Kevin left him there, blood in his beautiful blond curls, and went down to have breakfast. It smelled really good.

Chapter 34

A New Home

In the morning Rachael met Lily with a bruised face, which she had tried to cover with powder from a compact one of the girls had given her. Lily, eager to hear all the details of the dance, was anticipating an excited exchange.

"Happy birthday, Mom," was all Rachael could say before Lily drew close, lifted up Rachael's face, then gently pressed her daughter's head against her chest.

"What happened, Rachael, honey?" was all Lily had to say before Rachael's firm resolve to keep everything from her dissolved.

"Oh, Mom, it was awful." She buried her head in Lily's bosom and broke down. Lily could hear snippets of words and phrases through choking sobs. "I'm so sorry… I didn't mean to… I was just trying to surprise…"

Emma and Linda showed up at the screen door and were about to come in when Lily's sideward wave motioned them not to. They stood silently outside, watching, and then started back to their own cottage to light their little kerosene stove and make coffee. Lily watched them through the screen as they took one of the boys by the hand and led him away. But soon they were all back, sitting on the edge of the porch, sipping their coffee silently, listening as the story unfolded.

When I arrived at the camp Emma came out onto her porch and quietly called to me, motioning me into her cottage. She and Linda and a couple fellas were already there having coffee, looking very serious. The expressions on their faces scared me.

"What's going on? Is everything all right?" I looked from one face to the next. Linda handed me a cup of coffee.

"Yeah." She took a deep drag on her cigarette. "Yeah, everything's all right. You just can't go up to Lily's right now."

"Why not? There is something going on. Tell me." I looked at Emma and she looked down at her coffee. "Emma, what's going on?" I repeated, a little louder.

"John E., you can't go up there yet. Just listen to us." And Emma, with little comments from Linda and the two guys, slowly, gently unfolded Rachael's story of the night before. Emma and Linda kept touching my hands and my arms, trying to comfort me, trying to reach me in my bewildered state. One of the guys stood by the door, probably so that I couldn't rush out. I just sat there, trying to absorb what they told me.

Finally I realized I had to help her. "I need to see her. I need to be with her. Can't I go up? You can come with me." Emma and Linda looked at me, then at each other, and then back at me.

We walked up the path and paused just within view of the window but no one was looking out. Two guys who had been sitting on the edge of the porch gave us a concerned glance.

Rachael was at the table with her arms around Lily's waist, sobbing and talking and hugging Lily so tightly it looked like Lily could hardly move. When Lily tried to get up, saying she had to start the coffee, Rachael held her tighter and begged, "Don't go." Lily patted her head. Finally Rachael let Lily loosen her arms and Lily put the big percolator on. Then she got out the only bottle of whiskey she had and poured a little into a glass and gave it to Rachael.

"Here, drink this. It's medicinal; it will make you feel better." Rachael took a sip and coughed. She grabbed Lily again, but this time less tightly.

"Don't you worry, honey. We'll take care of you now." She watched through the screen as the two guys got up from the porch. Talking together in low tones and nodding their heads, they went by us down the path.

Lily went on, "We need to go see Sister Margaret." Rachael wailed at this, burying her head again in Lily's dress.

"No! No! I can't. They won't like me anymore. They won't want me there. I'm just poor white trash now. I'm no good. I couldn't be a nun now!" Rachael's voice was reaching a higher and higher pitch.

I felt embarrassed to be hearing this most personal interchange but still I stood silently with Emma, listening.

"Is that what you think of us? That we're poor white trash?" Lily asked quietly.

"No, that's not what I mean." Rachael tried to explain. "I just can't be perfect any more. They won't trust me – I slipped out and I was punished for it."

"Geezus, you have strange logic, girl. God doesn't punish people like that. This wasn't your fault." Lily turned back to the stove to pour two cups of coffee and bring them to the table.

"You were trying to do a good thing. God's not going to punish you for that, and neither is Sister Margaret or anyone else in town. You were a victim, don't you see? It's Not–Your–Fault." Lily emphasized her gentle yet firm words.

"Honey," she continued, "I've been thinking about this and I don't know if I can take care of you anymore."

With renewed sobs Rachael put her head into her hands. "No! No! Don't say that! You're my MOM. You're all I have left."

"Sister Margaret is your aunt, and she loves you almost as much as I do, and she would do anything for you too." Lily was also crying now. "You don't think I want to do this, do you? I'm just afraid for you and I just want the best for you. What can I give you here? What will you grow up to be? But Margaret can help you, maybe even get you into teachers' college. You could have a good life."

"I wanted to be a nun, like her." Rachael dripped tears into her coffee. "I wanted to join the convent."

Lily sucked in her breath sharply. "Oh. Well." She hesitated for a few seconds. "I don't think that's out of the question." She pulled off the dish towel she had tucked around her waist as an apron and started to dab Rachael's eyes.

"No, they'll never want me now." Too drained to shed any more tears, Rachael let Lily dampen the towel and wipe her face gently. Lily patted it, trying not to press on the bruised spots, and smoothed her hair.

"Don't you worry. Lots of imperfect people make their way just fine in the world, and even into the convent." Lily sighed and Rachael took the towel and continued now to wipe her own face. "And besides, you're perfect to me. You always will be."

Linda came up behind us and whispered, "Should we go in?" Emma nodded and we knocked softly on the door before we entered.

When Rachael saw me her eyes filled again, and she got up quickly and rushed into her bedroom. Lily just looked at me with a sad expression, shaking her head slightly. We all sat down at the table as Lily poured us coffee.

That was one of my worst years, the year Rachael lost her innocence and the year the United States went to war.

Jenny's Way

Part 3

Chapter 35

Career

Rachael finished her senior year living at the convent, explaining that the nuns wanted to send her to college and special preparations were needed to get her ready. That's what they said, but I thought I knew the real reason. None of her old classmates saw her, and I rarely did. But just before she left for college we met and I asked her if she would want a farmer for a husband after she became a college graduate. She threw her arms around me and whispered in my ear that she'd love a farmer if I still wanted her.

A bunch of the men at the mill had joined the armed forces, leaving the mill understaffed. I worked there as much as I could, and when I wasn't there Harry had me farming. Now that I was out of school I was working all day at either the mill or the farm. Without discussing it, I understood: Harry was trying to keep me busy and closer to home. I wanted to join the army like so many other guys, but Harry and Matilda insisted I was not only too young but needed at home. The war effort needed farmers too.

Harry was still spry and active, but I could see he wasn't as strong as he once was, or as limber. I understood farming. It was hard work but you were out in the fresh air, feeling the sunshine and hearing the birds. We had a larder full of food for the winter months so we generally were not subject to the vagaries of the marketplace. Our struggles were closer: a hot dry summer or a cold wet summer could mean the difference between an overflowing pantry and a scant one. The weather was our constant partner, affecting us for better or worse. We got by. It satisfied me just fine. I still put in time at the mill, but the farm was my future.

Harry had me doing everything. In addition to the regular chores I would paint the house, paint the barn, mend and paint the fences, move the outhouse, roof the chicken coop, pick up lumber from the lumber mill for repairs, and do any other job that struck his fancy. In the winter he had me prune the dozen apple trees, the grapes and the blueberries, and clean and oil tools and machinery. I'd plow the fields and seed them with corn, and then in the fall I'd harvest the corn into silage and reseed the fields with winter rye to plow under in the spring as green fertilizer. I was grateful that one year they decided to finish up the indoor plumbing and put in a tub, furnace, and indoor toilet. I helped with some of the work and the plumber adjusted his fees to give us a break. The farm was looking better than it had in years. It fairly sparkled.

Harry taught me how to worm the horses, trim their hooves, and harness them for plowing if the tractor wasn't available. He had me castrate and dehorn the goats and assist in the delivery of a calf. He taught me how to save the seed corn for the next year, storing it so it wouldn't mold. Matilda taught me to candle eggs and store them in isinglass, and how to brine pickles and corned beef. I learned how to sew on buttons, choosing from a large tobacco tin of savers Matilda had collected over the years. I learned to fry up eggs in the heavy iron skillet and how to clean, pluck and roast a chicken. Under the guidance of Harry and Matilda I could take care of myself and feed the family if hard times ever came, as they assured me they always would.

They kept me so busy, each season so brimming with seasonal chores, learning the techniques of good animal husbandry and the sensible farming principles that Harry's father-in-law had taught him, that I barely noticed three years had passed. It was more than a full time job. It was a way of life, in tune with the earth. Understanding how to counter the droughts, the wet times, the early and late frosts. Reading the clouds to see what weather was coming several days off. Noticing a particular insect that was eating the squash or corn or strawberries and learning how to protect the plants.

Chapter 36

Passing

The summer of that third year a stretch of good weather allowed us to cut the hay, dry it in the field, and bale it before any rain threatened to make it moldy. I was in the barn trying to fix the jammed baler when I heard Matilda scream.

Harry was out on the tractor, mowing the northwest field, when he realized something was radically wrong. He was able to stop the tractor, get off and start towards the house, and was almost to the back lawn when he collapsed. Matilda said she was washing out some overalls in the washtub on the porch when she looked up and saw him fall to the ground. She wiped her hands on her apron and yelled for me in a voice I will never forget, a deathly frightening scream. When I dashed out and saw Matilda rushing towards the field, my eyes traveled in the direction she was running and there was Harry.

Although we called the ambulance first, Doc Cremshaw arrived before it. Harry was limp but still conscious as we carried him to the first-floor guest bedroom. Matilda pulled up a chair and sat holding his hand, talking in a soothing, quiet voice, telling him it would be all right, as the doctor took his pulse and listened to his heart and asked him questions. Harry tried to answer but his words wouldn't come out right. He seemed confused. The doctor left the bedroom and motioned for Matilda to follow. I took her place, feeling awkward when she put his hand in mine. Harry was pale. His eyes, holding mine, looked frightened, and his mouth was moving rapidly as though he were speaking, but no sound came out. Matilda and the doctor stayed in the hall for a few minutes, talking in low voices, and then we heard the ambulance come.

The quick, purposeful and business-like way the ambulance workers handled Harry gave me confidence that he would be okay. But Matilda had me get the truck out so we could follow the ambulance to the hospital, saying that Dr. Cremshaw had painted her a grim picture. Harry was put in a small room with other patients in an area called intensive care. Their vital signs were monitored carefully and regularly as nurses in white dresses and starched white caps diligently came and went with purposeful. We watched him through the glass doors but we were not allowed to spend much time in the intensive care area. We went to the waiting room, and waited. At 6 p.m. I went out and bought us both sandwiches that we didn't want and coffees that we did. At 8 p.m. they told us we could go in for a few minutes and then we would have to leave. Harry had white pillows plumped up behind him. He was sleeping, pale and his breathing was labored. Matilda gently stroked his white hair several times and kissed him on the cheek before we went home.

At 10 p.m. we got a call that Harry had passed.

Harry had passed. Just like that. Matilda cried and cried. I hugged her and she soaked my work shirt with tears, and then she got up and put on a pot of water and made tea. We drank it together. She was in shock, I think. She talked about him, about what a good husband he was, about how they met at a barn dance and he was the handsomest fellow there and he said she was the prettiest girl. She pulled out a shoebox of old photos, taking them out one at a time, gazing at each one tenderly, describing the place and what they were doing when the photo was taken. One photo at the beach, another in the front yard, a comical one at the fair where they put their heads into holes in a painted panel showing Harry as a strong man in a leopard skin and Matilda as a maiden in lace with a parasol. By the time she tucked them all back into the box it was well past midnight. And then Matilda started to clean. She cleaned the kitchen, she stripped the beds and started washing the sheets and then she swept the bedrooms and the living room and the kitchen. It reminded me of Jenny all those years ago, cleaning the camp after her run-in with

Buck. I was tired, tired from the lateness of the hour and from the emotional toll the day had taken, tired from watching her work her way around the house. I wanted to sleep, but Matilda was just getting started. She was saying how people would likely be coming over so she had to make some sandwiches and deviled eggs. I finally fell asleep on the couch, but she was still going. In the morning I found her tucked into the sheets of the guest bed, and I understood she probably wasn't able to face the bed they had shared for fifty-four years without Harry in it.

Harry, the man who gently guided me, who had been true north in my moral compass, was gone. I now realize and am grateful for all the quiet wisdom he imparted to me over the years, but on that day I felt a fluttering in my chest as though a sheet had gotten loose in the wind. I knew I had to be strong, for myself, for Matilda, and for Harry. I wasn't feeling the strong confidence I needed but I hoped that just by acting it strength would follow.

Chapter 37

New Starts

I knew Matilda was a strong woman. She would have moments when she would break down and cry, but mostly she just went on, not quite as frisky as she once was, but still Matilda. I kept the farm going and I know I was a great comfort to her, just being there, just keeping things up, someone to cook for and clean for and look after. She would talk about Harry now and then, sometimes sounding angry, sometimes just sad, sometimes happily remembering times they'd had fun together. She said would see little mannerisms of Harry's that I had developed and somehow that seemed to please her more than any of my efforts to make up for her loss.

Matilda leaned on me more, not only pulling on my hand to rise up from crocheting in the easy chair, but for farm decisions and remembering those little things like how long the seed corn should be dried. I was grateful for the years Harry spent with me, sharing his knowledge of the land. I became the farmer.

"Do you know how much you look like Harry?" Matilda's eyes moistened with emotion. "I watched you walking back from the barn with those two buckets and I thought for a moment it was Harry." She hugged me and gave me a peck on the cheek.

I was filling in for Harry and I was filling in for Steve. Occasionally I thought it was unfair. Did she see me for who I was, or was I just the fill-in guy? That feeling was rare. Usually I was too busy to feel sorry for myself or think about how hard I had to work. When I saw other families struggling and people working day after day at the mill, I felt I was lucky to have what I did. I was lucky to have had such a kind and gentle man to teach me about life.

One day about a year after Harry passed, Lily stopped by. Matilda welcomed her like an old friend and they chatted over tea with juicy gossip and news that they hadn't shared for ages. Matilda asked Lily to stay for dinner, and Lily said yes. As we sat around the dinner table Lily started talking about the camp, which was not doing so well. The war rationing had been cutting into the donations that the girls got, and with so many of the fellas overseas they had been living pretty thin. The war made times tough everywhere, but at the farm our biggest problem had been getting new tires for the truck. We were able to feed ourselves and help feed some of the poorer families in the village.

After Sharon moved out to get married and settle down with a guy from a few towns over, business dropped off even more. Sharon once had a few fellas, but had been favoring that beau, and finally he married her and set her up in a little house near the garage where he worked. Now, with a kid, she was a regular housewife and loving every minute of it. When she left with her little bag full of things, Lily noticed she had taken the picture Jenny had given her, and she knew that Sharon would never forget the years she spent at the camp. No one in that new town blinked an eye when Sharon went to the market or passed by the bar. No neighbors said a word. Most thought she was as respectable a woman as any.

At the camp a teenager from town came up for a while, mad at her parents and wanting to be part of their little society, but Lily took her into her own cottage and didn't let her meet any of the guys. After a few days of talking to Lily and having her fill of chopping wood and using the outhouse, she took Lily's advice and went back home. Her parents asked no questions and were overjoyed at her return. Of course Lily had told one of the visiting constables about the situation and had him notify her parents that she was being kept out of trouble and to expect her home in a few days. The parents, taking the constable's advice, wisely stayed out of it. Their daughter returned, happy to be back in a comfortable home, and her parents learned to relax their rigid ways.

Lily always had stories to tell about who was going up to the camp and who wasn't anymore.

Then Lily told Matilda about Emma and Linda. Linda got some kind of fever one day. She started raving and they couldn't get her temperature down. One of the guys drove his truck down to the bottom of the hill, just above the descent to the cottages, and they carried her up and rushed her to the doctor's as Emma sat holding Linda's head in her lap and trying to protect her from too much jostling on the dirt road. Linda gradually got better, but she was weak, and when the flu came around that winter, it took her. Emma was inconsolable. Lily said you could have heard her wailing all the way in town.

Emma was still there with Lily, but there weren't many customers. Sometimes a few guys came up with some food and some beers and they'd all sit around and play cards like in the old days, but those times were getting less and less frequent and Lily was getting worried that soon they wouldn't have anything to eat.

Matilda listened to it all. She patted Lily's hand and shook her head in commiseration. Then she looked at me and I could almost read her mind.

"Lily," Matilda said. "Lily, what do you think about moving down here with us? We have lots of room and plenty of food. Of course you won't be having all the fun you have now, but you'd have running water and an indoor toilet."

Lily raised her eyebrows. She looked aside as though considering this proposal. A little tear welled up in the corner of her eye. She looked back at Matilda. She looked at me. I shrugged.

"It's all right with me," I said smiling. "I think it's a good idea."

"But what about Emma? I couldn't leave her there to shift for herself."

"Well of course she could come. She's welcome too." Matilda's tone was expansive.

"Well, let me ask her," was Lily's reply. But she was beaming, relishing the idea. "You two are just the finest people..." She tried to steady her trembling lower lip, and got control. "Don't worry. We'll carry our load. We're hard workers."

"We weren't worried for a minute," Matilda said. Then we sat around the table looking at one another and feeling as self-satisfied as if we had just solved a world-class problem. The more we sat and nodded our heads, the more we found reasons that this would be a good thing. Matilda pulled out a bottle of brandy I had never seen before and wiped off the dust. She poured a little into three glasses and we sat and smiled and toasted the future.

Chapter 38

Settling In

Within a week Matilda and I had the bedrooms set up for Lily and Emma. Lily was to bring the only piece of furniture that had any meaning to her, the big bed. We moved the single bed from my upstairs bedroom to storage in the barn. I moved into the bungalow out back, the one where Harry and Matilda had started out their lives together. We settled Lily into my old bedroom. Along with the bed she brought some pictures, her crucifix and Bible, a few articles of clothing, and Jenny's cast-iron frying pan. We set the bed up and she sat bouncing on it like it was for sale and she was trying it out. I gave her a hammer and nails and let her hang things as she pleased. She had two pictures in little frames that went on the dresser, one of Jenny standing with her hands on her hips, looking for a challenge, and the other of Rachael glancing back over her shoulder smiling.

We moved Emma in the next day. We hadn't wanted her to stay up at the camp alone but she said she needed that time, that last day to say goodbye to the camp and its memories. She didn't have much either: a few pictures, books and clothes, and a dress that had been one of Linda's favorites. She said she was thinking of making it into a pillow or a quilt if Matilda would help her. Emma got the small guest room at the back of the house. She said she didn't mind. It seemed even larger than their cottage, and with roses on the wallpaper it was far lovelier.

The next weeks were busy as the new roommates learned the daily chores and routines and the requirements of the animals and crops. They took right to it. Emma loved the animals. She was stronger and could clean out the henhouse and stalls and move bales of hay and buckets of water. Lily wasn't as strong but she was handy with a hoe, and soon learned to keep the kitchen garden free of weeds, hill up the beans and potatoes, and side-dress the corn with aged manure that Emma would haul over in a wheelbarrow.

The place fairly buzzed with women cleaning, hoeing, washing and ironing. The cooking was a joint effort. One would wash and snap the beans while another peeled the potatoes or apples, and the last one would churn the butter and wash, salt, and mold it.

Matilda's life was easier, and more fun. Lily's and Emma's lives were not much easier, but they certainly had fun too. Someone would drop by for a dozen eggs or a couple quarts of milk and it would turn into a gab session. Sometimes a few of the fellas who used to visit the camp would come by in the evening and start a poker game in the kitchen, but Matilda shacked them out before midnight. If anyone did sneak in and visit later, Matilda didn't know about it. Mostly it was a pleasant life. Even with the hard work we always had time for a cup of tea or a break when everyone went out to see the new litter of kittens or sat on the white slat benches in the garden during the evening, listening to the robins' evening song and the peepers in the distance.

They'd all go off together to the grocery store and the library, piled onto the bench seat of the old truck that Matilda had finally learned to drive. No one took notice of them or treated them any differently than anyone else. Lily had worried about it and dreaded they would, but it never happened.

They told some of the fellas that they could use the camp for fishing or whatever. After all, it wasn't really their property; they'd just been squatting there. Once in a while one of the guys would tell them he'd been up there and one of the cottages was leaking and mice were moving in and it smelled bad. Lily's cottage was still looking good and Tom Hadley moved in up there for a while when he had a fight with his wife. After a week of roughing it he decided to go back and see if they could get along. One Saturday night a bunch of mill workers decided to have a poker game and party up there and a small crowd showed up, almost like the old days.

Sometimes they would find a bum up there, or teenagers necking. But mostly it went unused. They talked about having weekend fishing parties, and maybe even getting together and buying it and making it into a fish and game club. They talked about bringing the big kitchen stove back down, but never got around to it.

News arrived that the war was over. We took down the brandy and had a glass and everyone who stopped in was excited and giddy and each got a glass of our homemade dandelion wine. We were all elated. We went down to the station about a month later to welcome some of our boys home and we threw them a big party at the rod and gun club.

Chapter 39

What Happened

As more people stopped by the house for eggs or milk or pickles or gossip, we pieced together the story of the night Rachael was raped.

The morning when Rachael told Lily what had happened, the morning of Lily's birthday, several of the girls were around and some fellas still lingered about. They sat outside while Rachael tearfully told her story. The word spread like wildfire. The guys got together and went to town. I wanted to go, but they pushed me back to stay with Rachael and Lily, telling me I should take care of them. Rachael was like their daughter. They had seen her grow up, seen her blossom. Not one of them would dream of touching her. No one would even imagine trying to date her, and now this punk had attacked her, attacked their beautiful, innocent, Rachael. They wanted revenge.

I got as much of the story as they would share. They said they started at the bars, going into the ones they knew Kevin hung around, asking if anybody had seen him, but it was morning and they were almost empty. Then they went to the soda shop and the bus stop, asking kids they'd seen him hanging out with. They went to the store where he bought cigarettes and to the package store where he stood around hoping to get someone to buy him beer or brandy. No one had seen him since the previous night. Finally they went to Lucille's. Jack Mason went to the back, to the kitchen door, and he could see Kevin sitting at the kitchen table, eating a big breakfast as though he were famished. Behind Jack were almost a half dozen others. Kevin didn't see him. When Jack pounded on the door Kevin nearly fell off his chair. He hesitated for a second, the gravity of the situation finally registering. He stood up rapidly, knocking the chair to the floor, and bolted for the front door.

Some of the fellas had anticipated this and were out by the street, coming up the front steps as Kevin emerged at a run. They grabbed him. Jack pulled up his pickup and five guys picked up the squirming Kevin and shoved him into its bed. Two more got in the front next to Jack. The guys in the back held down the struggling Kevin, who was screaming at the top of his lungs. Jack pulled quickly away and took the fastest route out of town. If anyone heard Kevin's screams they didn't say or seem to give it much of a second thought. The neighbors in the other side of the duplex, used to loud shouts from the Hunt house, ignored the commotion. The fellas came back that evening, solemn and quiet. Each went to his home and cleaned up and had a drink and went to bed. No one spoke of it again. No one saw Kevin again, anywhere, ever. He had disappeared, and no one missed him.

The next day, when Lucille didn't bring Michael to school and the nuns couldn't contact her, one of the nuns stopped by the house. It was unlocked, the front door ajar. She entered, calling Lucille's name, then Michael's. She walked through into the kitchen, calling out. The back door was open. On the table was a plate of crumbling half-finished dried-up eggs, and bacon with grease congealed on it. One of the chairs was knocked over and a fork was on the floor near it. She got a frightened feeling and crossed herself. She put her head out the back door, calling again. Then she went upstairs. When she first saw Michael, in a puddle of dried blood that had oozed from his head, it was obvious to her he was dead. She backed up so quickly she almost fell down the stairs, but grabbing the railing she was able to steady herself, although she wrenched her shoulder. She ran down the stairs and called the police.

This was the biggest happening in the town in more years than anyone could remember. The police called it a double homicide and said Kevin was the suspect, but Kevin couldn't be found. They questioned the neighbors, they questioned Kevin's friends, they questioned the nuns, they questioned the people who worked in the places Kevin frequented. They questioned everyone. No one knew where he was or what might have happened to him, and if anyone suspected, they didn't let on. Kevin had never treated anyone, even his friends, with anything but contempt. No one liked him and no one seemed to care if he disappeared. Of course the police believed he had run off, that he killed Lucille and Michael and went into hiding—took a bus, bummed a ride, walked away, left town. No one talked about the attack on Rachael. The police kept looking and asking questions, but the answers just didn't come. Sometimes they suspected that people knew more, but if they did no one talked about it. It was as if the history of a whole evening and day in that town had just been swallowed up and never happened.

Lucille and Michael were buried next to Buck. A large crowd came, some for curiosity, but most because they were touched by the nearness of it. A small town was mourning as one, as a single entity. Two murders, a mother and son, and the second son, probably the murderer, missing. Many women wept, not just for this family but because of the tragedy of it. Most of them didn't know Lucille or Michael or Kevin or Buck, but by then they had all heard the story. It was their own story, a story of hard work and hard lives, of trying to keep a family together and find some happiness and enjoyment along the way. A story of fathers passing down the abuse that had been passed down to them, of mothers trying to make the best of it and ignoring what they could no longer control, of families protecting each other even though they knew they were wrong, and that one of them was indeed evil.

They were buried together, and months later when the carver finished the stone, it said simply, Gone On To A Better Place.

Chapter 40

Shifts

Lily and Matilda started going to church together. Emma refused to go, saying the church didn't want her and she wouldn't have anything to do with a religion that wouldn't accept all love. Matilda would drive the old truck, sitting so low you could hardly see her over the steering wheel. They'd bounce down the bumpy road together, attend Mass and visit with some of the other church ladies afterward, and then bounce all the way back laughing and talking like a couple of teenagers. They acted so silly it was beginning to seem like they had somebody special at church, maybe a beau or something.

After a while Sister Margaret started dropping in, first for tea, lingering longer and longer as she got into deep conversations with Lily and Matilda. Then she'd come by for dinner and the kitchen would be buzzing as they whipped up a good homemade meal. During these times I would sit at one end of the table and Sister Margaret at the other, both Lily and Matilda flanking her. If Emma could have gone to another room without insulting everyone she would have, but she sat close to me and ate with her head down, focusing on the meal and ignoring the conversation about God, religion, and the New and Old Testaments.

Then one Sunday about a year after Lily and Emma had moved in, the kitchen was fairly electric with excitement. The day before Matilda had had me catch and kill one of the young turkeys for dinner. She plucked it and the next day the kitchen smelled like heaven, all warm and delicious. Freshly baked bread was cooling, the turkey and stuffing were in the oven, and pies sat on the counter waiting to go in once the turkey was out. There were mashed potatoes, beets and squash; it was a Thanksgiving meal a couple months early. The women were rushing around trying to time this feast to be ready at 5. Lily was particularly excited and ordered Emma around one too many times. Emma finally snapped back at her, "I'm not one of your handmaidens!" whereupon Lily apologized and told her how much she appreciated her help. Emma smiled back and they resumed their frantic cooking and table-setting. I was staying out of the kitchen and busied myself with cleaning out the stalls. Every now and then Matilda would yell from the window for me to bring in one thing or another.

The last time she called to me, she looked me up and down and told me to "get the damned cow shit off you before the company arrived." Leaving my boots on the porch I went through the dining room to go upstairs, and I noticed not just one extra place setting, but two.

I washed up, put on a fresh shirt, pants and shoes, combed my hair, and joined the ladies in the kitchen. Matilda smiled her approval at my modest transformation and immediately sent me to bring up a bottle of sherry from the cellar.

I returned with the sherry just in time to see a big black car come into the driveway and Sister Margaret and Father O'Reilly step out. Father O'Reilly, still tall even with a slight stoop and a cane, looked distinguished, with a full head of white hair. So this was what they were all abuzz about.

Matilda had laid out some delicate glasses on the buffet and instructed me to pour sherry and offer it to our guests and to Lily and Emma. Emma, who did not like to drink alcohol, declined, but the rest of us sipped the sherry until Matilda and Emma had all the dinner on the table. I ceremoniously carved the turkey. Before Matilda started to serve the side dishes Father O'Reilly stood up and said a short grace, then raised his glass. "I want to thank Matilda for this lovely dinner, and I also want to officially welcome Lily, who will be entering the convent in the spring."

I'm sure some of us sat there in stunned silence with our glasses raised and our mouths open. I offered my congratulations. Matilda fairly beamed. Sister Margaret leaned over and put her hand on Lily's.

"My dear, my only niece," she began, with equal measures of pleasure and solemnity, "I've been praying for years that this would happen."

Lily smiled and looked modestly down at her plate. "I don't know if I deserve this, but I will be very happy to join your convent."

Everyone toasted, even Emma, who raised her water glass but had a puzzled look on her face.

After the meal Father O'Reilly looked at me and said, "I remember you. You were something of a devil when you were young, weren't you? I'm glad you ended up here and straightened out." I nodded politely, but could only think that years of good behavior amounted to nothing, and one misdeed was all he remembered. What does that bode for people who make mistakes? How can you ever recover a good reputation if people remember only that one transgression? I answered him, "Yes, I was lucky." But I find myself going back to that moment many times in my life. If you were really bad most of your life, you could be redeemed by one striking act of goodness, but if you were good, a silly error in judgment marked you for life. How fickle we are, how judgmental, how like lemmings, all believing alike with few questioning the views of the many.

Chapter 41

And Then

Those five years ago, Lily and Sister Margaret decided it would be best if Rachael boarded at the convent. I courted her there, before she went away to college. It was hard because the nuns kept her secluded, but I would send notes and letters and she would reply, cautious and welcoming at the same time. I would not find out until later why she was so secluded.

The next fall, with the financial support and encouragement of the nuns at the convent, Rachael entered a local teachers college where she boarded, working at any odd jobs she could get when she wasn't studying. I saw her only rarely during that time, but continued to write her. When she graduated and returned to the convent school, they happily accepted her as a teacher. Once when she came back during a college break, I saw her at the local market picking up something for the convent kitchen. Now and then they allowed her to come up to the farm for a couple flats of eggs and a few gallons of milk and we would get to visit for a little while, but mostly she stayed at the convent. She returned from her last year at college a beautiful, poised and intelligent teacher. She continued teaching for the nuns, the favorite of every schoolboy from first grade to eighth.

I could not imagine ever being interested in anyone else in my whole life, and I knew she felt the same way. It was like a story, like a fairytale: we were made for each other. The only cloud that was still hanging over us darkened one afternoon when she invited me to tea with Sister Margaret. I was hoping this would be the time I could speak to them both about marriage. Wearing a suit, I showed up at the convent and was led into a small sitting room where Sister Margaret and Rachael were already seated. They greeted me formally as another nun quietly came in with a tray of tea and treats for us. Sister Margaret poured tea and Rachael offered me cookies. I had imagined myself dashingly requesting Rachael's hand, but now I felt awkward and not at all in command of the situation.

Sister Margaret started the conversation. "John, we need to discuss a delicate matter with you." I nodded. "I'm not one to mince words much so I'll get right to the point." She paused to sip her tea. "Do you remember when about five years ago Rachael experienced that unfortunate event?" I nodded, shocked that we were discussing that terrible day. How could I ever forget it? Why, when I thought we had put it all behind us, were we going to dwell on that? When Sister Margaret started to speak again Rachael put her hand over mine and with a finger signaled her to wait. She spoke next. "John E., I had a child." She stopped and searched my face. I know my hand trembled. I was afraid to pull it away, feeling in shock. I just sat there, looking from one to the other. "I knew it." I paused. "I had a feeling, but why didn't you tell me?" Sister Margaret answered, "That was my doing. I thought it would be better if no one knew."

"Yeah, but..." I started to respond. Sister Margaret interrupted. "I know. You were her boyfriend, her special friend, someone who cared more than anyone else, but it was a difficult time and we ourselves weren't sure what to do. Knowing or not knowing would not change the outcome. She had a son. You could not have changed that. You could have moved on, found another girl, but would you have?" I looked back and forth between them, and my gaze stopping on Rachael's face. She looked scared. I shook my head. "No." A little tear ran down Rachael's cheek.

So there it was, and when I asked her again if she would still have a farmer for a husband she didn't hesitate. She said she would be the luckiest woman in the world to be married to me. Sister Margaret whispered a little 'Hallelujah' under her breath, smiled and put her hand over both of ours.

"Now for the hard part," Sister Margaret began again. "You can leave Jerome here to be cared for at the orphanage, or you can, as a couple, adopt him." I hadn't met the boy. What a decision. I looked at Rachael. She was very pale and her eyes had a pleading look. "Well," I started, "if it's up to me, there is no question." I paused for emphasis, "Of course we'll keep him." Rachael let out the breath she was holding and smiled brightly at me. Sister Margaret beamed.

As much as she could, Rachael left the past behind her. The nuns helped her to see the sad life Kevin had lived and gradually she had only pity for him, and was able, eventually, to forgive. The townsfolk helped, as a group, never mentioning it around her, never treating her any differently than before, except maybe even more gently. She said that was harder than if they had shunned her, she had held so much guilt. I had difficulty understanding how she was able to put it behind her. But she showed me how our present was so good that it overshadowed and finally swallowed up the bad parts. She said she'd had enough pain and sadness in her life. She accepted it, and was ready to move on and be happy.

Our wedding was bigger than I was prepared for, but the nuns and priests wanted to offer a full church as their gift to us and so the pews overflowed with black habits and flowery hats. It seemed like half the town came. Rachael was beautiful. Half a dozen of the nuns served as her bridesmaids, all marching solemnly in front of her down the aisle, hands folded in prayer, smiling and nodding to friends in the pews.

Lily walked Rachael down the aisle, looking proud and smiling broadly. Sister Margaret sat in the second pew next to Matilda. Sharon and Emma sat behind them.

The four-year-old ring boy was our oldest son, Jerome, whom I adopted the next month. It was Rachael who had named him after his grandfather, Buck. He walked carefully down the aisle, the rings tied to the pillow he held stiffly in front of him, looking uncomfortable in his new suit. He managed to arrive at the altar without trouble, with the familiar and loving nuns close by and his mother following. He tripped on the way out, but two of the nuns took his hands and swung him between them the rest of the way and out through the doors. He had started laughing and left the pillow in the aisle.

The reception in the church hall was a wonderful collection of pot luck dishes brought by the nuns, our friends, the parents of Rachael's students and other townsfolk. As a shy and quiet farmer, I was still bold enough to ask Rachael to dance to the tunes the little group of local musicians began to spark up, and after a few glasses of wine the floor was bouncing with couples, all celebrating Rachael and me. Kids danced and ran around the couples until they collapsed or their parents swatted them. Elders sat and watched, pointed, laughed, whispered and occasionally rose for a quiet waltz. A guy from our class got a little tipsy and swung Rachael around until she deliberately sprang loose to where I was positioned, and I stepped in to sweep her into a gentler pace. She was tolerant of the "silly boy," whom she treated gently, like one of her students who might need some extra attention.

After we were married she settled into the bungalow behind the barn with me.

Rachael was pleased with her life. A generally happy woman, sometimes she had a furrowed brow or irritable word and when I probed we found at the bottom of it the guilt she was still fighting back over that one day. She seemed to torment herself more over her dishonesty that night than over the rape, which she said she remembered little of. But all in all, her life was weighted heavily to the happier side. It was better than she could have imagined, with the satisfaction of teaching children and seeing the delight of understanding as they learned. She was a wonderful teacher.

I always felt lucky to have landed the perfect grandparents and best wife. Matilda said luck had nothing to do with it. I had a beautiful wife, a fine home, and a good solid job. Hard work on the farm ensured us food for the rest of our lives. But there had been many days when I had thought we wouldn't get to this point in our lives, so many bleak days and worried nights. Although I'd had an inkling about Jerome that first year Rachael had been secluded at the convent, I was afraid to bring it up, afraid of the truth. But I've found that when you shine a light on the truth, it's nowhere near as fearsome as your imaginings. If Rachael could manage to accept it, to move on and forgive, she wanted me and everyone to. Matilda could see the worry in my heart and would explain in her own way how it had all turned out for the best and we had only to make an effort and let go of the rest.

It was just as Harry used to say: there was only one gal for me.

Chapter 42

The Secret

One year on Jenny's birthday, the customary dozen roses did not show up on her grave. Most people didn't notice, but Rachael did, and we all started to speculate. We remembered the man in the big black car, and the beautiful gravestone and granite urn on her grave. Who did this, and why? Then in a flash Rachael remembered the vice president of the mill, who had just died the previous month. She wanted to know more, and in a move that for her was strangely forward, she visited his home.

A maid answered the door, invited her into the foyer, and went to summon the owner. A man came down to meet her.

Rachael explained who she was and that she was Lily's daughter and Jenny's granddaughter. At that point she realized she might have put everyone in an embarrassing position. The man blanched but recovered quickly, and she was relieved when he smiled, invited her in, and requested coffee for them both.

"Yes, I knew your grandmother. She was a very special woman." He paused when the coffee came and poured unsteadily, spilling a few drops before he handed her a cup. "Do you know the story?" Rachael shook her head no. "Well, when your grandmother was in school, she used to help my mother do some cleaning around the house. When my mother, Lizzie, got sick, Jenny used to come and care for her. By that time, I think, she was living up on the lake. We offered to give her quarters here. She declined, but would come and give the kind of care that no one else seemed to be able to." The man paused, bowing his sleekly combed dark hair towards the coffee cups he was refilling, "My mother and father trusted her with everything, and she never let them down. No one else could make Lizzie comfortable or soothe her as Jenny could. Jenny was with her when she died. My father was very grateful to Jenny, but she never told anyone about it and would never accept more than the few dollars she thought was owed her." He paused to sip his coffee, looking at her intently. "My father never forgot, and had that handsome gravestone erected on her plot and ordered flowers every year. Now he's gone, and I forgot to have the flowers sent."

Now it was Rachael's turn to look intently at him. "I've never heard that story. My grandmother never told me, and my mother didn't either. Strange that it never came up."

"Indeed," was all he replied.

Rachael thought he might be hiding something. She thought he looked familiar somehow, but she could not place him, and the smooth manner with which he addressed her told her that any secrets were unlikely be revealed here.

Rachael thanked him, saying he didn't have to worry about the flowers anymore; she was just glad the mystery was solved. He walked her to the door and waved as she went down the steps, but when she got down the hill and looked back, she saw him still standing in the doorway.

Jenny's Way

Part 4

Chapter 43

Moves at the Farm

The first years after Rachael and I were married were full of changes.

After a year of honeymooning at the bungalow we decided to move back into the house. Emma moved out to the little bungalow, preferring the quiet and solitude, saying it suited her. She took with her the few mementoes she had from the camp. With Lily's help she had made the dress Linda once wore into a pillow, and it lay on the little settee. She was never without the little gold-filled pinkie ring Linda had given her all those years before. Worn too thin in places to stay on her finger, it now hung from a chain around her neck. That bungalow had seen so much of my family on the farm, first Harry and Matilda, then Rachael and me, now Emma. It stood on the dirt drive just a little up the hill, nestled in the trees and positioned so that it was cool in the summer but in the winter had the pleasant south sun shining across the porch and through the windows. The road was rutted during the spring thaw, but by summer the tractor had smoothed it out.

Now and then Emma would come down for dinner, and she helped with the farm chores. She'd clean out the chicken house and bring in the eggs, but wouldn't tarry too long afterward. Some called her a recluse, but we knew she just had her ways and her world, and they were different from ours. Every week or so we'd see a visitor, Sister Ann, as Lily was now called, walking up the dirt road. On occasion Sister Margaret's car, driven by Lily, would wind slowly up the road. Emma told us the 'black crows' were stalking her, looking for a fresh body, but she said it in a joking way so we knew she liked it.

Matilda moved down into the guest room Emma had left, saying she just didn't want to do the stairs anymore. She said she liked it because it was close to the kitchen, the bathroom and the back door, so she knew all the comings and goings. In the morning she'd have the coffee brewing and bread baking and a pot of water heating for tea before anyone even stirred. So we woke early to the kitchen smells. But Matilda was also the first one to bed, and we would have to tiptoe around the kitchen after she retired. And if we happened to have a rousing pinochle game at the kitchen table, she would appear and grumpily scold us.

Rachael and I moved into Matilda and Harry's old room, palace-sized compared to the small bungalow bedroom. We splurged for a new mattress, since I think the other one had been there for thirty or more years. Lily and some of the other sisters at the convent made us a pretty quilt in exchange for some of the produce, eggs and milk we sent there. We felt we were rich.

Jerome had a small room upstairs, near our room. There was another bedroom upstairs that we used when, a year after we were married, we had our second son, Steve.

We explained to Jerome that he was going to have a new brother or sister. He ordered a brother, but a sister was his second choice. He got the brother he ordered and seemed pleased to have him even though he was a lot younger. He'd peek into the crib and talk to the baby, telling him how they would play baseball and go fishing, and parroting what I said, that he couldn't wait until he was big enough to help in the hay field.

While Rachael was at the school Matilda helped look after Steve, and she tried teaching Jerome some of the garden and chicken chores. Sometimes I'd put Jerome up on the tractor with me and we'd plow for a little while, before he got tired of it and got down to see what Matilda had for him to do. Jerome was often off by himself, rough-housing with the dog or digging holes in the garden. This 'garden work,' as Matilda put it, was annoying, and she'd scold Jerome as she fixed the holes, but he'd disappear before she'd finish filling them and the scolding would turn into sour muttering. Sometimes, if Matilda was particularly busy, she'd put Steve in the swing attached to the clothesline as she hung the clothes out because, she said, she couldn't watch both of those rascals and do chores too. Luckily Emma was there to buffer her from the boyish exuberance.

Rachael would get to escape the boyhood ruckus at the house, walking quietly down to the school each morning. As much as we welcomed the extra income her teaching job brought in, Matilda and I were looking forward to summer recess, when we'd have that extra pair of hands. But that break came and went and soon we would have one more little mischief-maker.

Chapter 44

Harvest

Harvest time was always busy and stressful. Everyone worked from dawn to dusk and beyond. We would send the boys out to pick up apples and they would almost always come back covered in apple mush after throwing the rotten ones at each other. Steve, still small, took the beating. Although Jerome had a good aim he rarely started the fights, and never used the full strength of his throw. Steve, at three, instigated these apple tosses and wouldn't back down until the sting of a yellow jacket that had been gleaning the fruit's sugar brought the fight to a swift and painful conclusion. We'd hear Steve hollering as he ran back to the house, seeking a vinegar and baking soda poultice from Matilda.

Matilda and Emma would can fruits and vegetables all day, keeping the kerosene stove on the back porch busy and lining up the jars to cool on the porch railings. The apple pies they'd cool in the house, away from cats and kids and flies. On Sunday we'd get out the old crank ice-cream maker and the kids would take turns cranking. Adding vanilla ice cream to the cooling apple pies sent everyone into swoons of gustatory pleasure.

Jerome was sent to clean out the root cellar, a particularly dirty job that Steve was still too young to help with. Jerome would evaluate what remained there. Anything that it might still be good went into a basket for Matilda, who would cook it for dinner or send it out to the pigs or compost it. Then he'd wipe down the shelves and rake up any debris, put the baskets on the lawn to be rinsed and dried, and leave the door open to air it out.

The combination of older, long stored food and the abundance of fresh food provided our evening meals with dishes heaped with mounds of hot and cold selections. We ate until sated and what leftovers there were went to the animals. Dogs, cats, pigs, chickens, all enjoyed the harvest.

Steve, still too small to be much help and adept at avoiding chores, was assigned daily egg duty and other menial tasks that might keep him out of our hair. He was good at bringing messages from the fields back to the house and coming back to the fields with water or tools. And he was always around when I needed to do an emergency fix on the tractor. Machines fascinated him.

Before harvest season was a time when repairs were made, fences inspected, hoses replaced, plumbing checked, kindling bins filled. Soon winter would arrive, and being unprepared was not an option if we and all the critters were going to survive. The barn stalls were cleaned carefully and fresh bedding put down. Once a freeze came it would be very difficult to clean out mounds of frozen manure. I used the tractor to spread the manure on the fields that would produce next year's grazing and hay. Most of those fields were farther from the house so the ripe smell of freshly spread manure would waft home only when the wind was just right. I was teaching Jerome how to drive the tractor and how to take the wide turns when dragging the "honey-wagon" around the corners of the field.

One oppressively hot afternoon in late August, Rachael brought a picnic lunch out to the field I was working in far from the house. The driving heat was making it almost impossible to continue working so I was grateful for the rest. I'd been trying to fix a waterline that went out to that field where no pond or other water was accessible to the cows. I was still sweating over the pipe connected to the old claw-foot tub we used as a watering trough. Rachael laid out an old blanket and unpacked several sandwiches and pieces of pie and a thermos of swizzle. She came up next to me, bending over to examine what I was working on. "Geeze, you stink," she said as she gave me a shove towards the tub. My balance was off enough so that even as I thrashed my arms about in an effort not to fall in, I couldn't avoid it. As I fell I grabbed her arm, laughing, and pulled her in after me. The water was cool and refreshing. I leaned back to immerse my head and rinse the sweat off, sliding further under her as she straddled me. The picnic lunch was going to wait.

Chapter 45

The Farm Fills Up

The June after our fourth anniversary Rachael again gave birth. After a long discussion we named our new dark-haired daughter after her great-grandmother Jenny, but she was a replica of Rachael, sweet, good-natured and quiet. Why were we naming our children after dead people? My father Steve had died when I was still in high school, and we never heard why. He was just found dead near the train station where some bums hung out. Jenny was gone almost nine years now. And yet we still decided to do it. Matilda approved. Even though she never mentioned Harry's name, we were sure it went through her head, why not Harry? Why Jenny? Why Steve? Why Jerome? None of them had come to a good end. Were we tempting fate? I guess we wanted to believe this connection to these people would somehow help to right the ill-fated paths they had found themselves on. Silly dreams.

By the time Jenny came along Steve was getting big enough to dress himself and get around well. Jenny and Steve kept Matilda hopping. But Emma continued to help out with the kids and cooking and the other chores so that Matilda wasn't too overburdened. Matilda kept saying that having the kids running around helped keep her busy and young.

Jenny was as sweet as Steve was cranky. We were pleased to find her even-tempered and generally happy. Jerome started grade school the second year after Steve was born. He wasn't the best student, getting average grades. We told him we thought he could do better while trying not to make him feel bad about his grades. His first year in grammar school he grew quite a bit so his clothes perpetually looked small. We heard that the kids were teasing him but the sisters would protect him when they found anyone being mean to him. Of course with Rachael teaching and all the students adoring her, the pressure to be a special student fell hard upon his shoulders, and we wondered if he would be up to it. Some afternoons I'd watch them walking together on the road up the hill to the farm. From the high vantage point of the tractor I could see this big awkward-looking kid kicking a can up the road, and a lithe and graceful woman next to him carrying a satchel of books. She'd say something to the boy and they would both laugh. When she saw me she'd wave and he'd wave too and start running home.

Having Jerome at school helped take pressure off Matilda and Emma. We had more time so we were able to put in a bigger vegetable garden and start keeping a few more pigs and even a couple beef cattle. We were able to put away some cash, feed ourselves, feed others and put food by.

By the next spring Jerome was big enough to help me cut, carry, split, and stack enough wood for our next winter's supply. By the time Jenny was toddling around we all had a regular routine and the farm was running like a machine.

We could see Matilda slowing down, but Emma would come down early in the morning, before most of us were up, and help her with some of the morning chores, bringing in firewood, starting the stove, filling the big kettle full of water. We still had that old kitchen stove; Matilda wouldn't allow us to go to gas or electric. Hard as it was, with our help she kept it cooking autumn to spring. Once it got into summer and the kitchen would get too hot with the woodstove going, we would move out to the back porch, where a kerosene stove was set up. I screened in the porch and on some warm nights we even ate out there.

I always think back on these times as some of the most fulfilling of our lives. Everyone was healthy and we had plenty of food and enough money. Do you know how it feels when everything is going well and you start to worry anyway? You think somehow you're tempting fate by having everything so good. These were the strange things I would dwell on then.

Chapter 46

Fast Friends

Emma's move to the bungalow seemed to feed her need for solitude, but sometimes she seemed too reclusive even by our tolerant measure. At those times Rachael would send Jerome back to Emma's little cottage to bring her a piece of cake or ask her to join us for dinner. Sometimes Jerome would come back pulling Emma by the hand, and other times he was sent back with only an empty plate and a thank you.

Then Emma started frequenting the local library. She'd come home with two or three books, saying she'd have gotten more but she couldn't carry them. After a while Jerome would go with her and help her carry the books back, sometimes staying at the bungalow with Emma for hours while she read to him.

Emma began coming to dinner with us more often, and she and Jerome would describe in detail the latest book they were reading. I'd never seen Jerome so animated, so excited. His heavy brow, inherited, we supposed, from his biological grandfather, lifted with enthusiasm when he talked about a character or a scene. His favorite books were adventure and animal books, and he would vividly describe Jack London stories of the wild North Country.

Gradually Jerome's grades improved. Arithmetic was not one of his best subjects, but his English and geography and history marks were better, and the nuns said his attitude had changed. He was less sullen and more engaged, and the better his grades became the more he interacted in class. He became more outgoing. He even had a few friends, who would come over for dinner or go fishing with him.

Steve was starting school and we loved to watch the two of them stroll down the road together. With funds we had from selling two piglets we bought Jerome a bicycle, and he would ride the bike down the hill to the school with Steve on the back rack. On the return trip home they would both trudge up the hill, Jerome pushing the bike, not yet strong enough to ride it up.

I took them fishing to the same fishing holes where Harry had brought me in my youth. We'd pack a lunch and come back with a nice dinner of trout that Rachael would ooh and aah over, making us all feel like we were indeed the finest fishermen in town.

One Sunday we had a short day of fishing when Steve, using a throw line to tease a bite from the reluctant trout, threw vigorously and hooked himself in the leg. The hook penetrated deep into the flesh. I tried to push it through so I could cut the barb off and remove the hook, but the skin was tougher than I imagined and Steve screamed loudly. We ended up going back down into town. I had Steve on my shoulders, the hook close to my face, the line cut off. Fortunately old Dr. Stanley, now retired, was home. Except for the mean sting of the liberally applied iodine Steve had no more pain once Dr. Stanley injected some Novocain and pushed the hook through the skin to cut off the barb and withdraw it. Steve had been brave until the tetanus shot set him to howling. He limped home and bragged about the event for weeks until we were all very tired of hearing about his exploit. Finally Jerome told him that if he ever did that again we'd leave the hook in. After that we didn't hear much more of the incident.

There was always something happening at the farm. New animals were born and old ones nursed along. We had one old cow that was pregnant and too old to come back into the barn with the other cows. Jerome noticed her missing and gave me the news in an alarmed tone. He recruited Steve to go out and look for her, and they found her lying down far in the back of a field, chewing her cud as though this were a most natural thing. The boys brought her out fresh hay and silage and water every day. They worried about her when it was raining and made an extra trip to make sure she had enough food. I thought we would have to put her down when she finally calved. To my surprise, with the help of the boys she clumsily dragged her heavy frame up and dropped a sizable female calf, then went to work cleaning up the new baby. We used to call her Sophie, but after that Jerome started calling her the 'Indomitable Sophie,' and that stuck. We never bred her again, but let her come and go out to the pasture with the other young cows. Matilda said I had too soft a heart for a farmer.

When time and chores allowed them to get away, Jerome started to bring Steve up to Emma's. Emma bought each of them a compass, a magnifying glass, and a jackknife. When not reading books aloud to each other they would go for walks up into the woods behind the bungalow, where Emma would show them how to search for salamanders and box turtles, and what wild plants were safe and good to eat. They'd call these outings their expeditions. When they'd come home to dinner those evenings they'd pretend they had been great scientific explorers who had discovered some magnificent new creatures. They would them give quasi-scientific names like Rachaelitca Flowericus for a pretty flower or Jenniferous Germicus for a mold growing on tree bark, upon which Jenny would start to whine that they were picking on her.

These were as hard as our times were then. We'd lose a chicken to the fox, or a machine repair would take up too much of my time, or maybe Rachael would have to stay late to give a student extra tutoring. Sometimes we had droughts, but the crops survived, and other times we'd have floods and I'd have to worry about mold. So simple our lives seemed.

Chapter 43

Bad Break

We almost lost Matilda when she made a misjudgment on the back steps. Trying to shoo a cat away from the birds with her broom, she slipped and fell off the step. An odd twist sent her down onto the ground with a startled scream. She lay there with her leg in an awkward position, her hip broken. Fortunately Emma had been out at the garden, close enough to hear the scream. She stood up from the row of beans she was cultivating and saw Matilda on the ground, whimpering, one arm flailing about, the other clutching her hip.

Emma came running. She could immediately see Matilda's hip was broken. She rushed inside, called the ambulance and grabbed a blanket to cover Matilda, who by now was sobbing. Emma felt helpless. I was, of all times, not at home but at the hardware store. When I arrived home to an ambulance, flashing lights and men in white coats bustling around, a feeling of panic engulfed me. I had a sense it was Matilda. Everyone except Matilda, Jenny and Emma was at school. Just then Emma came rushing out to me, Jenny in tow, frantically trying to explain what had had happened. The ambulance workers came around the side of the house with a stretcher. Wrapped up tightly, looking pale and small, white-haired Matilda reminded me of Jenny all those years ago.

"I think I broke my hip," she said in a shaky, frightened voice. "Now I'm done for," she finished, shaking her head, a tear running down her cheek into her ear. Emma took out her handkerchief and dabbed at Matilda's face as the men from the ambulance prepared the inside to receive the stretcher.

"I'll follow you down in the truck," I said, but the ambulance workers said I should wait, that it would be some time before we could see her, that they would be taking x-rays and making her comfortable. I nodded, and letting go of her hand I told her we would be down after Rachael and the other kids got home. She nodded back at me, taking in a few fearful gulps of air, trying not to cry outright. Emma, Jenny and I stood there watching as the ambulance pulled out and rushed down the road, Jenny waving feebly after it.

We went inside. Emma looked lost. I had her sit down at the table with Jenny while I put the kettle on for tea, gave Jenny a glass of milk and, with my back turned to them, took out a couple of small glasses and the brandy tucked away on a back shelf. I poured some for Emma and myself and handed her a glass. With little hesitation she started to sip, with Jenny still beside her. I gave Jenny another glass of milk while I waited for the tea water to heat. Emma sat there, looking dazed, shaking her head slightly.

"Damned cats," was all she said.

"Don't feel bad, Emma. It's not your fault." My words didn't seem to reach her. She still focused on the glass, spinning it around between her fingers.

Jenny, getting bored, asked to go out. She knew to stay on the farm, and we allowed her to roam freely on the property. She left, screen door slamming after her, and we could hear her out there, swishing the broom around and yelling repeatedly, "Damned cats! Shoo!" Emma and I looked at each other and smiled. The spell was broken.

"Well, I guess I'd better get some supper started." Emma finished the last of her brandy, got up, poured water for our tea, then went to the cellar to bring up potatoes and start the meal.

She began scrubbing potatoes while I did a few kitchen chores I'd been ignoring. As she scrubbed and I sharpened the knives, we talked about the days at the camp when things were fun. We rarely talked of those times, but this unfamiliar turn of events churned up memories and gave us license to reminisce.

They seemed so far away, those days. She reminded me of things I'd long forgotten, and I told her the perspectives of Harry and Matilda, and those of the town. We laughed over one silliness or another. We got angry over the injustices, then sad over the losses. We had tea and then another glass of brandy. I helped her prepare the chicken and cut up the turnip. We were quite gaily into the dinner preparations when I heard Rachael and the kids come in the front door. Emma and I stopped, looked at each other and felt the sting of remorse as we realized how grave the situation was for Matilda and how wrapped up we were in our shared past.

Rachael came into the kitchen as the boys raced upstairs to fling their books down and change their clothes. Her gaze went from one of us to the other, as we had paused in our chores and in our guilty confusion turned to look at her. She could see immediately something was amiss. "Where's Matilda?" I went over to her and asked her to sit down as Emma turned back to filling a pot.

"She's had an accident," I said as Rachael, her brows knitted, looked from me to Emma and back to me. "She fell off the back porch. We think she broke her hip. She's at the emergency room."

Rachael sucked in her breath and uttered a little shocked "Oh."

"They said they needed to take x-rays and evaluate her and there was nothing we could do down there, but we could visit her later when she was more comfortable." I tried to make it sound like we were not just standing around having a good time while Matilda was alone and in pain at the hospital.

The boys tromped down the stairs, and we sent them out to pick string beans for supper. "Check on Jenny while you're out there. Make sure she's okay," I hollered after them.

Rachael started to help with the supper preparations, setting the table and pouring out milk.

"I'll watch the kids while you both go down, okay?" Emma was always up to giving us a helping hand.

The boys returned, Jenny on their heels. "You wash and snap the beans. There's hot water and salt pork in the pot on the stove waiting for them," Rachael directed the kids.

And we all cooked and ate dinner and discussed Matilda's fall, and what we were going to do.

Chapter 48

Recuperation

Rachael and I drove the truck down to the hospital in Norwich. We talked about what we might need to do if we could bring her home, and what we might have to do if we couldn't. She was close to ninety now. We were worried about her frailty, but we couldn't imagine what we would do without her. She was the heart of the home, just like Jenny was the heart of the camp. Things seemed to dissolve once that heart was gone. Matilda might not have been doing a lot these days, but she kept the tea water boiling, swatted the flies and did some of the simpler cooking tasks. She often schooled Emma or Rachael on the finer points of making fowl stuffing, coleslaw, dill pickles or jelly. Matilda barely even went off the porch to pick a flower here and there. She wasn't able to kneel to weed or bend to rake. But she was our heart. With her diminishing eyesight she would read what she could of the newspaper and then recite what she'd read at the dinner table and start a discussion, which was often peppered with her strong opinions. The problems with the government, local and otherwise, the problem with youth these days, with religion, with commerce and education – nothing was off limits. Almost any topic was one on which Matilda had a strong viewpoint, and usually a sensible solution. We often told her she should have run for office, but she pshawed us, saying she was too honest to get elected, and we had to agree.

All these things ran through our conversation as we drove to the hospital. The idea that she might someday be gone was of course a possibility, but not one we had often confronted. A home needs that anchor, that heart, that central person who helps guide the moral compass of the family. Both of us now pondered this in silence as we drove. Who would that person be? Who would step in to fill that void if Matilda no longer could?

We wouldn't have to wait long to figure that out. When we arrived at the hospital and went to the information desk, the receptionist looked through her roster of newly-admitted patients, peered up at us over her glasses and said, "So, you're the family who belongs to that loud and feisty old lady?" Rachael and I glanced at each other, smiled and nodded yes. "She's resting now. She's in wing B, down the hall to the right. Take the elevator at the end to the second floor. She's in room 204." We thanked her and headed up to Matilda's room, grateful that she was still well enough to be memorable.

Even before we entered Matilda's room we heard moaning. Someone seemed to be in pain. In the bed closest to the door was a white-haired woman, the source of the sound. A curtain separated her from Matilda. Peeking around it we found a nurse helping Matilda lean forward so she could put a pillow behind her. Matilda's leg was hanging from a sling. "Can't you fix this contraption? I can't roll over or get comfortable." Matilda seemed to be trying to get the nurse to somehow make movement easier. The nurse said she couldn't lower her leg because it needed to be immobilized. "Well, at least give me some aspirin so that it doesn't hurt so damned much." The nurse said she would get some painkillers. Matilda saw us and said, "Where have you been? I expected you hours ago." We were surprised to see how lively she looked. "I wish you had brought me some supper. The food here is terrible."

On her way out the nurse stopped by the moaning patient's bed and spoke to her, plumping up her pillow and offering her water.

We had visited with Matilda for an hour when the doctor came in and wanted to discuss her treatment. "You can talk to them in here. I'm not dying and I want to know what's going on." Matilda was going to be boss even here. We looked at the doctor. He nodded and told us that it was a serious break, one that often didn't heal in such elderly patients. We could put her in a nursing home where the hip might heal over time, or we could take her home and try to tend to her there. Maybe it would heal, but she would likely be in a wheelchair for the remainder of her life. He was sorry it wasn't very good news. We thanked him and we each took one of Matilda's hands. She pulled her hand away from me and used the sheet to wipe her eyes. "I knew it was going to be bad, but I don't want to spend the rest of my days in a nursing home. Don't make me go there." She looked at us pleadingly.

Rachael and I looked at each other. "Don't worry, Gram, we wouldn't put you in a home." Rachael, patting her hand, was the one who answered. "But we have to find out how long you need to stay here before we bring you home, and what kind of special help you might need once you get there." Using her free hand Matilda covered her face and started to sob, relieved that she'd be going home again. I bent down and hugged her and kissed her forehead just as the nurse came in with the painkiller. "Don't you worry now, sweetie," the nurse said. "You're going to feel much better once you take this pill." Matilda obediently took it with several sips of water and quieted down. "I know I ain't going to live forever, but the closer it gets, the harder it is to let go." We both nodded, but realized we probably would not fully understand the sentiment until we were at the point Matilda was.

Chapter 49

Home

After several weeks, far longer than we had expected, Matilda came home. The hospital arranged to have a special bed set up in her room, with a sling and a crank to raise and lower different parts of it. They taught us how to help Matilda use the bedpan, something she called that "damned cold crap pan." They taught us how to move her and wash her. Emma was the main caregiver. For some reason Matilda was more modest with her family than with Emma. But it was Jenny who surprised everyone. She participated more and more in Matilda's care. She would sit with her and ask Matilda to read to her. She would bring her water or go for Emma if Matilda needed anything she couldn't handle.

Rachael would come home from school and poke her head into Matilda's room, then go out to call me from the barn, and we would both steal a glance at the old woman with her spectacles and shaded light, reading to the young girl who sat on the bed, leaning to hear every word. Matilda, animated, held the book up now and then so Jenny could see the pictures and then went back to reading in a somber or excited tone, both of them concentrated on the story. Emma and Jerome would carry their own library books for the week and an additional pile for Matilda and Jenny.

When Matilda wasn't reading to Jenny she would brush Jenny's long dark hair, and sometimes braid it. Or Matilda would tell Jenny stories of her youth or of my childhood, and Jenny would come to dinner bursting with questions for me and Rachael. We became concerned that Jenny wasn't getting out enough, that she was spending too much time with Matilda. But by the time we thought we should talk to them Matilda was able to move around more, and at her last doctor's visit she was able to graduate to a wheelchair.

The doctor came and removed her cast and several nurses helped her out of bed. Even though we had tried to move her around while she was in bed, they said she had lost a lot of muscle tone and would be stiff and have a few bedsores. We got a wheelchair with a specially padded seat to take some of the pressure off her bottom. Matilda moaned and cried when they moved her from the bed to the chair. They left us with a special sling that attached to the bed so we could get her in and out of the bed ourselves. After a few days of what she called agony she was looking better, and started to wheel the chair around by herself. Jenny still helped her, but they were no longer confined to Matilda's bedroom. Some days they'd be out on the back porch, some days in the parlor. I built a ramp from the back porch to the ground, and Jenny, who was growing daily, would wheel her to the garden, where Matilda would explain how to tend one plant or another.

In the fall when Jenny started school, Matilda was on the front porch, waving and smiling, but with a handkerchief close to wipe away the tears. Jenny ran back several times to give her a kiss on the cheek. Finally Matilda had to shoo her away and tell her how wonderful the new school year would be.

Matilda was on the porch when Jenny came back up the hill with her brothers, running and waving and dropping her new books and her lunch box as the boys followed her and picked them up.

Emma helped Matilda and tried to fill in for the loss of Jenny. They would read together when no chores or cooking had to be done. During supper preparations they would talk and talk. Matilda was able to roll up to the kitchen table, her legs in the wheelchair underneath, where she could help chop and peel, and she was happy to feel like she was back in the family circle once again. She'd start whistling "When the Saints Go Marching In" and Emma would chime in, then they would both start singing loudly, sometimes drumming on the table.

Jenny would come home and have a snack with Matilda, tell her about her day at school, then go upstairs to change before going out to play with the new kittens. After supper Jenny and Matilda would do the dishes and talk more about the day and the news.

Matilda was not strong, but she was more able to help herself. She could now shift from the wheelchair to the bed or a chair or to the toilet and back. One evening when Rachael and I came in from weeding the onions we thought it was too quiet, and when we went into the parlor we found Matilda in the big easy chair and Jenny squeezed in next to her, both asleep with a book on their laps.

Chapter 50

Storm

Matilda wasn't the only one on the mend. In previous years the dam above the mill had fallen into disrepair. During a dry period timbers, stone, gravel and clay were brought in and work got underway to fix it. What no one expected during that dry time was a storm of such magnitude that it would threaten the work.

We were lucky to get our hay in just before the rains started. Repairs to the roof of the barn and the bungalow would have to wait.

Heavy rains began and went on for a couple of weeks while the workmen rushed to complete the job. When another storm hit, a hurricane, we knew there would be trouble. We heard that the Eagleville dam on the Willimantic River had collapsed and we went down in the wind and rain to watch as the waters rose and workmen frantically tried to protect it with sandbags. We saw the sandbags begin to wash away, and gradually more and more of the new timbers were torn out and tumbled downstream. Finally the north angle of the dam washed away and Little Flats was under water once again.

The dam was gone, no longer holding back the beautiful lake we all enjoyed. The Shetucket ran like the river it had always been. The boats that had been pulled up onto the shore and had not washed away were now sitting on a deep beach that dropped to the chasm where the water was channeled to the mill. Just above where the dam had once been, caught behind the embankments that still stood, was all manner of debris— tires, old bicycles, the rusted remains of a wood stove, a wringer washer with the enamel still white and only a little rust around the edges, a rusted wheelchair, even the rusted hulk of a car.

What a mess in town, with sand and gravel piled up below the bridge. The town was lucky this time that the bridge held, but our beautiful lake was gone.

Emma walked up along the fishermen's path and then told us what a catastrophe the site was. What was once a lake was now a river a hundred or more feet out from the cottages. The receding water had left a muddy hole, where some animals were making the most of the freshwater clams stranded at the high-water mark. She could see shells that critters had left behind. The smell was awful.

The cottages were high and dry, although one of them had the roof torn off. No longer on the lake shore, they looked oddly out of place on the edge of a field of mud and stone. Some debris from upstream was caught at the little peninsula where the cottages stood. She said she didn't think people would be going up there anymore except by the Jenny's Way dirt lane, since that fishermen's path would fall into disuse and soon fill with brush and brambles.

At the farm we were lucky. One area of the west cornfield was flattened by the wind and driving rain, but we were able to get most of the corn in that fall. The barn roof had a leak that the boys and I repaired, and we re-roofed the bungalow. We were grateful that Emma came out now and then with lemonade and swizzle, cautioning us to be careful not to fall off the roof.

There was damage to the chicken house, which blew over and scattered chickens everywhere, but we were able to stand it up again and Jenny rounded up all but two of its dazed inhabitants.

The apples that were blown off we collected and made into cider or apple butter. Some harvesting had to happen earlier than we could prepare for, so a few things went bad and the pigs got more in their troughs than they usually did.

During the storm we dusted off the kerosene lamps and dug out the candles. We hadn't realized how reliant we had become on electricity. We were lucky to still have a hand pump, and even an outhouse, though that needed the cobwebs swept out and a little work to make it usable in case of another emergency.

We talked about how we could manage if other emergencies were to arise, and we all worked on preparations to keep us safe and able to take care of ourselves and others.

We all agreed we were lucky, but our biggest loss was the beautiful lake where we had swum and fished and boated.

Chapter 51

Jerome

The boys were growing up. Jerome was in high school, a big fellow, bulky and strong. Physical education teachers sought him out for sports teams where his size would be a bonus to their games. Muscular and well-built, he certainly looked like he could be a good football player. He had the strong features of his grandfather, and a scowl from him could put fear into his classmates. But to our great relief, Jerome wasn't interested in bullying, fighting, or sports. He wanted to study. He excelled in English, devouring all the books that were assigned and then seeking out others, always borrowing from the school library classics that the other kids shunned. We were surprised that he didn't seem very interested in girls, mentioning them only on occasion, and then only in regard to what they were studying together. He loved science too, and got an A in his biology class without seeming to study. Math was still not a strong subject for him but he passed. He not only avoided sports but actually appeared not to like them, complaining that the physical education teachers seemed to focus on him, hoping to bully or shame him into joining a team. That made those classes particularly uncomfortable.

He was a great help around the farm. His strength allowed him to lift and carry things and help in ways we never would have thought possible. Haying could be done in half the time. Cleaning the stalls and barn and chicken coop was easy after he did the heavier part, leaving us to do only the finer cleaning. He could hoe down a row of beans in minutes. He tossed around fifty-pound bags of grain like they were five-pound bags of sugar. Rachael and I would sometimes just stop and stare at this big handsome young man pitching bales and bales of hay up onto the top pile of the wagon like a machine, without tiring. Steve, in the wagon, had to work hard to keep up with stacking them.

Jerome was still going to Emma's bungalow, often studying there in the evening. He continued to walk with her down to the library and spend time reading and studying there, then help carry the books back. Occasionally Steve and Jenny would accompany them. Rachael and I sometimes talked about this longstanding relationship. We knew that without his early connection to Emma he might not have become the student he was now, but we worried that he wasn't making friends his own age and didn't seem interested in girls. We hinted at it to Emma, who only replied that they enjoyed the quiet time to read and talk and did not understand our implied concern. At Sunday dinners when we all gathered we watched to see any hint of an odd connection between them. But we didn't see it and decided they were both just shy people who enjoyed the quiet-time connection between them that they couldn't get when they were with others.

But still we watched.

We finally had to tell him we could not afford to send him to college, because as good as his grades were, he would not qualify for a scholarship. He seemed to have known this and was prepared for our talk about it. He said he was joining an agricultural group for young men that would teach him some of the farming practices we were not using and also some more modern farming techniques. Rachael and I were very relieved to see how much common sense he had and how well he understood our home and farm economics. So Jerome, like me, was going to be a farmer.

With his help and knowledge we would be able to expand the farm to some of the acreage that was still wooded and have more animals and crops. We didn't need to become a large farm, but for Jerome to someday have a family here with us, we would likely need to expand some. We were contemplating this, thinking about a future which seemed distant and yet, we thought, inevitable, when our attention to that topic was abruptly brought to a standstill.

Chapter 52

Matilda

One afternoon Rachael came home early from the school, saying she wasn't feeling well and was going to bed without dinner. Emma brought her juice, and Rachael asked for tea with lemon and honey too. She had a sore throat and thought it might be a cold coming on. Emma brought her the tea and some aspirin and tucked her in. Rachael went to sleep and woke up sneezing. Handkerchief after handkerchief went into the wash as her sneezing and runny nose lasted about a day before she started coughing. The coughing brought up ugly clots of mucus and blood, but she was relieved to have it come up rather than sit heavy in her chest. Gradually, after three days at home from school, she started to feel better. By then we all seemed to be coming down with it.

Matilda had been busy about the house, helping with laundry by putting it into the machine and then taking it out for Emma to hang outside. She was still peeling vegetables, snapping beans and even rolling out pie crusts.

The fourth day after Rachael came home sick from school was a Saturday, and she was feeling much better, relieved that it was the weekend. That morning Matilda didn't have the water on for tea. Emma went to her room and found Matilda sneezing and coughing all at once, her eyes red and rheumy. Emma made the tea and brought it to Matilda with lemon and honey just as she had for Rachael when she was first coming down with it. Emma helped Matilda to lean forward as she put pillows behind her and then gave her the tea. As Matilda started to sip it cautiously, not wanting to get scalded, she coughed and spilled tea on the bedspread. Emma rushed out to get a towel, and came back to help Matilda over to the wheelchair so she could clean up and go to the bathroom. Matilda could hardly move from the bed to the wheelchair. Emma wheeled her into the bathroom and helped her onto the commode, then went back to change the bedclothes.

Once Matilda was cleaned up, had on a fresh nightgown and was tucked back into bed, she looked better. Emma pulled up the shade and let the light of the just-rising sun into her room, and asked her if she needed anything else. Matilda said no.

By this time we were starting to come down to the kitchen. Jerome had gone out to milk the cows and Jenny to get the eggs. Emma told us that Matilda wasn't feeling well and thought she had the cold we had all been suffering from. We went in to see her.

A diminished Matilda was pressed back against the pillows, grasping the bedspread with both hands, and then leaning forward and gasping for air as though she could not get enough into her lungs. Forward and back, forward and back, using both her nose and her mouth to try to inhale as much air as possible, yet it was not enough. She looked at us, panic in her eyes, unable to talk, and when we asked if we could help, she could only shake her head no. We asked if we should go for the doctor, and again she shook her head no. Emma had some aromatic ointment and she rubbed it onto Matilda's neck and upper chest to see if it would help loosen up the phlegm that seemed to be choking her. That seemed to help a little. Emma went to start breakfast. By this time Jenny was back from collecting the eggs and was standing by the side of the bed, holding Matilda's hand and stroking her white hair. Matilda's eyes were on Jenny, and this seemed to calm her. Her breathing became a little less labored.

We left Jenny to stay with Matilda while we went to the kitchen to call the doctor.

When we returned Jenny was lying on the bed cradling Matilda, who looked relaxed but was still struggling to breathe.

"Don't be afraid. Don't be sad. It's time for me. I'm ready." Matilda took a breath every couple of words. "I love you all, but I'm going to join Harry." She stopped to take several more rattling breaths. "Jenny, remember I'm always here." She reached towards Jenny's heart, closed her eyes and sighed out a breath, and did not inhale again. Jenny continued to hold her, tears starting to run down her cheeks. Rachael and I could only look on, but finally told Jenny to let her go. Jenny kissed her forehead, and withdrew her arm from behind Matilda's head. She kissed her on the cheek and pulled the sheet up to Matilda's shoulders.

We all went out to the kitchen to call the doctor back and decide what to do next.

Chapter 53

Jenny

Jenny was being stronger than we had expected. Because of her calmness we thought she might be in a state of shock. She would cry for a while, and then get quiet. Before the doctor and mortician came to pronounce Matilda dead and remove her body, Rachael and Jenny washed her face, tucked in the sheets, and made her look good. Jenny snipped off a piece of her white hair, "to keep her with me always," she said. Rachael and I attempted to continue with our day as calmly as possible, trying to help everyone cope with this loss of our grandmother. The boys went in and visited her for a while. We did not need to light candles; the dawn was spreading sunlight throughout her room. But Jenny lit a candle anyway, "to help her find her way."

Matilda had stopped going to church after Lily entered the convent, preferring, as she put it, to "worship in her own way." None of us were regular churchgoers, barely attending even on the holidays that seemed to draw those others who were not very religious. But Matilda did have a sense of morality that seemed to be more respectable than that of some of the churchy people she'd criticize. She believed in fair play, honesty, kindness and forgiveness. She understood that the beauty she saw in her everyday life— the sunset, morning glory, dew on the spider web, even the snake in the grass— was a gift. Perhaps divine, perhaps not, but that awareness was a gift that pointed towards the spiritual and she absorbed and shared it all. When she sat with Jenny on the porch and listened to the evening birdsong her heart swelled, and she shared her joy in those moments with Jenny.

Jenny got it. Their long hours together were spent sharing the knowledge, sharing the secrets and mystery of life as Matilda understood them. The gift was given by the old woman and received by the young girl. Jenny had never been a regular girl, but now she seemed wise beyond her years. Jenny received the torch. She didn't run with it; she walked with dignity. She was still a kid, not yet a teenager, and still had the mischief of a child, but in her twinkling eyes we could see Matilda laughing through them.

At the service for Matilda, Jenny was in the front. She looked on the ritual with sad dignity, a tear now, a smile then, and a hug for everyone. Each of the kids put something into her coffin: from Jerome, Matilda's favorite book; from Steve a blossom from her favorite rose; from Jenny a candle and matches, again, to light the way. Jenny explained to us that Matilda was afraid of the dark and that's why she liked keeping the light in the bathroom on all night, and why now Jenny was going to be sure she wouldn't be in the dark.

We had all had such a scare those few years back when Matilda broke her hip. I think we had been preparing ourselves for this moment ever since then, silently knowing that it was inevitable and trying to get the most from every moment.

Emma seemed to be the most aggrieved by Matilda's loss. She wept in the background, quietly, her eyes puffy and red. She shook her head and said again and again how kind Matilda had been to her. We all tried to comfort her, which only seemed to embarrass her, and she would gently push us away and start to cry anew. Each of us in turn would put an arm around her shoulder or hug her or give her a handkerchief. Jenny walked up and took Emma's hand and led her outside the funeral parlor. I watched as she pointed to the bird singing in the tree nearby and they talked quietly. I could see the calming effect that Jenny had. The child had so grown into her great-grandmother. She whispered something into Emma's ear and they both started to laugh.

The days that followed were mixed with sadness and change. Gradually we started to clean out Matilda's room. It was very spartan and there was little to do. In her last years, even before she'd fallen, she had been paring down her possessions. She said she didn't think people should leave a lot of garbage to go through. She had a few pictures on her dresser, of Harry, Steve, Charlie and Mary, Rachael and me and Jerome at our wedding, and another of all the kids. There was very little to pass on, just a couple of well-worn books and a few pieces of jewelry. We gave a little locket we found to Jenny, who immediately put it on, having placed reverently into it the snippet of Matilda's hair she had saved.

We tried to get Emma to move back into the house, but she was firm in her desire to remain at the bungalow. Instead, Steve volunteered to move down to Matilda's old room. We were all surprised.

Chapter 54

Steve

So Steve moved out of the room he shared with Jerome and into his own room, Matilda's old bedroom.

With Rachael's dark hair and eyes Steve was becoming tall and lanky. Like Harry he was going to be handsome. But he was our question mark, our middle child. Someone once told us that middle children have it the hardest. The older child is clear in the mission to excel above the others. He is first, strongest, smartest, the best. The youngest would always be the baby, fawned on and favored in a different way. The middle child had to constantly prove himself, being neither first and best nor last and spoiled. Of course we always tried to treat them equally, but sometimes that was difficult. If one got an especially good grade in school or an award, or did something special, we praised that child. If one misbehaved or did something we thought unacceptable, we punished that child.

Jerome became a young man who did well in his studies, graduated from high school, and worked full time at the farm, which he would probably inherit. Jenny was becoming someone wise, kind and full of compassion; we could only encourage her. But Steve? He did not excel scholastically, barely scraping by with average grades. We were told he was a smart-aleck in school, sometimes loudly cracking jokes that disrupted class. When he managed to get a B we would praise and encourage him, but that only served to show what a small bit above average he was in his studies. He'd come home and go to his room to study, and sometimes we'd find him reading comic books or drawing pictures of cars. The teachers would talk to

Rachael about him, telling her he often didn't finish his homework, but when we asked him he said it was done. We tried to get him to show us the finished homework and a few times he did, but only a few. We offered to help him with any subjects he didn't understand or any studying he needed to do. But he said he was "getting it." Jerome's offer of help seemed to bring more stress to the situation. Steve resented that 'smart-assed brother' trying to help him – "What does he know?" We were surprised by the level of venom he had for Jerome and surprised by his language, which we would never use. After these outbursts we made him to stay in is room. Teachers would tell Rachael to watch which friends he hung out with, but she never saw them. He was sly in his movements around the school and around the town.

    We asked Jerome why Steve had so much animosity towards him, but Jerome didn't seem to understand it either, assuming it was because of his good grades. But he didn't think that was fair because he had worked hard and studied to get those grades, and he said that if Steve worked hard he could get those grades too. He also thought it could be because he might inherit the farm.

    Steve started to stay late after school and not come home with Jenny, leaving her to walk by herself. His excuse at first was his studies, and at least once when Rachael went to check up on him he was in the library with his friends, although it didn't look like he was studying. We didn't want to check up on him too often. We wanted him to think we trusted him. We wanted to give him the benefit of the doubt. Staying later after school got to be a regular occurrence and after a while when Rachael checked the library she usually didn't see him there. Now he said he was going to a friend's house to study. Once he gave us the name of a friend he was supposed to be studying with and we called the house. A boy answered and said yes, Steve was over there studying. We called the house the next day when he didn't come home to dinner and the boy answered again and with laughter told us to stop nagging him.

    Of course our concern was now acute. Our middle child, growing tall, thin and darkly handsome, was someone we didn't know anymore.

Then one day the high school principal call Rachael to his office. He explained that Steve had been cutting courses, that he was off school property during class, and rumors were flying about his bad character. Someone had seen him hanging at the edge of the school property smoking a cigarette. Someone else had seen him with some other boys passing around a bottle in a paper bag. Girls complained that he and other boys were taunting them as they walked by. Since Rachael's school was not in the same area as the high school it was hard for her to keep tabs on him. She thanked the principal, but came home in tears.

We were at a loss as to how to handle the situation. We felt we had tried to be fair and gentle in our dealings with Steve, but he was not responding to our kind treatment.

Alone together before bed, Rachael and I talked. "Do we now need to be more firm?" I asked Rachael, who was troubled that Steve didn't think more about her standing as a teacher, and how it might affect the family. "But how can we manage his time away from school if he doesn't come home?" Rachael felt helpless. I felt angry but didn't have any answers either. We'd never had to deal with this problem before.

It was a total embarrassment to Rachael, and to me. We had worked hard for what we had, struggling to distance ourselves from family histories that were less than upstanding. Was there indeed, as my mother once believed, a bad seed that cropped up every other generation? Did we tempt fate too much by naming our children as we did? All this and more we discussed privately in our bedroom that evening, as we waited for Steve to come home.

Jenny's Way

Part 5

Chapter 55

Who's George?

We needn't have waited up that evening. Steve never came home.

He didn't go to school the next day, either.

We wanted to call the police but were afraid to, afraid of the talk, afraid of the outcome. When we did finally go to the police department, they told us it wasn't uncommon for a teenager to go missing, that they run away, and come home once they are cold and hungry enough. Or if they went to a friend's house, the parents would get tired of having an uninvited guest with no idea as to when he might leave. Did we know any of his friends we could talk to? Did we know where he "hung out"? They asked us personal questions. We were to call them if we heard anything or if he came home, and they would call us if they heard anything. They told us not to worry. They seemed professional, but all we could think was that once we left the station they discussed our family and how we were raising our children, what our histories were.

We went home and called the only friend Steve had for whom we had a phone number. The woman who answered sounded angry.

"How should I know where he is?" she asked rudely, slurring her words. "They both took off, my son George and him. Damned kids. They took half of my groceries and a full bottle of vodka. They ain't just runaways, they're thieves too!" She snorted out this last remark.

"Well, do you know where they might have gone? Do you have any clue as to their whereabouts?" I was trying to be civil.

"Don't know. Don't care." Her voice was starting to rise.

"Mrs. Brady – your name is Brady, right?" I continued. "They could be in trouble, they could be in danger. Isn't that important to you?"

"Like I said, don't know. Don't care!" She uttered each phrase emphatically, and hung up.

We called the police and told them what we had found out. They said they would be watching for them.

Supper that evening was subdued. We told everyone what we knew. Jerome said he remembered George Brady, and that he was a troublemaker. Not a roughneck like some, but someone you couldn't trust, who smoked cigarettes and was sometimes caught drinking by the teachers, on and off school property. Jerome thought he might have been stealing too. Emma just sat eating quietly, shaking her head every now and then. Jenny listened, looking from one of us to the next as we talked.

"He's been bad," said Jenny. "But I don't think he's bad inside." Everyone nodded.

"Once there was a boy who used to follow me around. He kinda scared me. Steve saw him, and he pushed him up against the wall and told him to 'lay off' of me. And that boy did. He left me alone after that. I don't think Steve's bad inside. I think he's just sad." Jenny finished off this sentiment with a mouthful of mashed potatoes.

"Really?" Rachael asked, ignoring the 'sad' remark. "He helped you with a boy who was bothering you? Why didn't you tell us about that?" She sounded annoyed and a little scared.

"He took care of it. I didn't have to. It wasn't that important." Jenny was matter-of-fact.

"Does this happen a lot, boys bothering you?" Rachael wanted to follow up on this.

"Now and then," Jenny said, and took another mouthful of potatoes. "Guys just like me. What can I do? I'm just friendly to everyone." Jenny's shoulders went up, dimples showed and her eyes twinkled.

Rachael and I looked at each other, trying not to show what we were thinking. Were we raising a bunch of children we didn't know anymore? What was going on? Was Jerome, the only one we were really concerned about from the beginning, now the only one who appeared sound, or was there a secret hidden story there too? Steve seemed out of our control and Jenny seemed naïve.

We looked back at Jenny, just now realizing that, as a child almost entering her teens, she looked older and acted more mature than her age, and was pretty and going to be a beauty. We had much more to worry about than we had imagined. Jerome's eyes went from one of us to the other, knowing exactly what we were thinking.

"Aw, don't worry," he said. "She's only a kid."

Emma, silent, just watched us all.

But our worries had just begun.

Chapter 56

Cracks

On the fourth day Steve came home. It was late in the afternoon. From her vantage point in the garden Emma saw him go into the empty house. She came into the barn to tell me.

I rinsed my hands in the bucket beneath the outside pump and went into the house. I could hear him rummaging around in his room. I sat in the kitchen, quietly waiting for him to emerge.

After about ten minutes he came out with a couple of bags which looked like they were full of clothes and other personal items.

He stopped dead in his tracks when he saw me sitting at the table, facing his room. He almost dropped one of the bags, but recovered it before it fell. I got up and went to the sink, drew myself a glass of water and drank it. Then I started to heat water on the stove. All the while he just stood there. I leaned my back up against the sink, crossed my arms and asked him if he wanted a cup of tea. He looked confused.

"Why would you want to have tea with me?" He regained his composure and became confrontational. "I'm the bad boy, remember?"

"Who said that? I never said that. Your mother never said that."

"Yeah, but you're thinking it now. Mrs. Brady says we're just a bunch of thieves. George stole her vodka, you know?" It seemed like he was probing, looking for me to tell him what I thought.

As the tea water started to heat up I heard Rachael come in the front door.

She walked into the kitchen and dropped her books onto the table, "OH, THANK GOODNESS you're okay!" She sounded so relieved. She stepped around the table to give him a hug.

Just then Jenny came in the front door and Emma and Jerome came in the back, all converging in the kitchen.

"STEVE!" Jenny exclaimed happily.

"GET AWAY from me!" Steve was flustered now. His plan to slip in and slip out unnoticed was ruined. Everyone seemed happy to see him. How could he get away? "I hate you all! Just leave me alone!"

Rachael and Jenny stopped moving towards him, both with shocked and hurt expressions. "How could you say that? We love you." Jenny's response was weak but sincere.

"You are nothing but hypocritical jerks." He swung his head around to include all of us. "YOU, you're the biggest jerk of all!" He nodded his head towards Jerome. "Do you know how you got here?" Steve hissed this bitter remark at him and then glanced towards Rachael.

I could see where this was going and rushed around the table, pushing Jenny and Rachael out of the way. Before I even knew what I had done, I hit Steve back-handed so hard that it knocked one of the bags out of his hand.

Everyone stood there in stunned silence. I had never hit anyone in the family like that before.

Steve recovered the quickest. This was what he'd been hoping for all along. "See, I knew you hated me. You're all a bunch of hypocrites." Then, nodding towards Emma he shouted, "You're a queer!" And nodding towards Jerome, "And you're a bastard of a rapist!" He picked up the bag and looked at Rachael. "And you know we don't even have to talk about what YOUR mother was…" He turned and walked towards the front door. "Go ahead. Ask them." He looked back over his shoulder at Jerome as he left, slamming the door.

We stood there in stunned silence. No one tried to stop him. Jenny was the first to move. She walked to the front door and watched him walk down the hill with his bags.

Jerome was the first to speak. "What does he mean?"

Emma took the now wildly-whistling tea kettle off the heat. She pulled a chair over to the refrigerator, stepped up on it, opened the top of the crock and took out an old, crumpled package of cigarettes. She stepped down and went out onto the back porch and lit a cigarette. We all followed her except for Jenny, who was still standing at the front door, looking down the empty road.

Chapter 57

History Lesson

When I think back on all the paths we take in our lives and how they affect our future, I am mystified by how any of us turn out to be good decent citizens. How does it happen? Two people with the same parents, in the same conditions, same food, same school, same family, and yet they can become so different. Maybe I never believed in Steve. I wonder about how I acted. Did I treat him differently? Maybe. But he was a different person. Each of them was different right from the moment they were born. How could I help but treat them all a little differently? If someone is interested in science, you reinforce that interest; if they are interested in music, you reinforce that interest.

I didn't think I favored one over the other; I just worked to support their interests. Both Jerome and Jenny were more studious, more interested in school, and I encouraged that. Steve wasn't good in school. I barely knew what he was interested in other than comic books, drawing pictures and cars. Cars. Who did he get that from? No one in our family was interested in them. Was it my fault? Rachael's fault? What should we have done differently? I wanted to run after him, to grab him, hug him and shake him and tell him that whatever was going on with him he didn't need to keep it from us. I wanted to ask him what he expected me to do. I felt that it wasn't just our fault, that he wouldn't let us in either.

I think I noticed from an early age that he was different and that we didn't understand him, and he didn't want us to know or understand him. Always we were kept at arm's length. What was beneath that exterior, beneath that quiet surface he showed us? There was more, but he didn't allow us to see it. Rachael thought it was his inner judge, as she called it, that he was judging himself more harshly than we would have, that he was judging himself instead of trusting our judgment, that he thought if we knew what his inner thoughts and drives were we wouldn't like him. So he pushed us away before we could push him away or judge him. But he was a harsher judge than we were.

Now that boy who we thought would grow out of it, who we thought would find an interest that he could build a life on, was gone. That boy who we thought would find himself and learn to trust us—that boy was gone. He was gone and we didn't know when, or if, he was returning.

We were all hurting. Emma withdrew to the bungalow. Jenny hid in her room with her books. Rachael and I blamed ourselves. But the person who would have the most difficult time was Jerome. We knew we were now going to have to tell him. We were not only afraid to tell him his parentage, but more worried that he might not trust us, that he might accuse us of keeping it from him or lying. After Emma went to the bungalow and Jenny went upstairs, we sat Jerome down at the kitchen table.

"The first and most important thing we want you to know is that we love you," I started out. "And that everything we've done, we thought was for the best. You may not agree, but it's hard, even in hindsight, to know what is best, or how one can do things better."

Rachael spoke. "When we were married your father adopted you." She reached across and put her hand over mine, and with her other hand took Jerome's. "When I was a teenager, even younger than you, I was raped. By some stroke of chance I became pregnant and I had you. It was the most important day of my life, and I loved you even before you were born, and I never stopped loving you." She paused to get up to start water for tea. "Your father and I didn't get married right away. I was still in school. The nuns sent me to college to get a teacher's certificate, and while I was there they raised you. Do you remember when your father and I were married? You were the ring bearer. We were so proud of you."

Jerome sat taking it all in, looking at his hands, sometimes looking at Rachael, then at me. "So you're not my real father?" I shook my head and replied, "No, I'm not your father by blood, but I think of you as my son, my firstborn."

"So, who is my father?" That question – for years we'd worried about and dreaded hearing it. Rachael tried to explain. "He was a boy who lived in town and went to school with us. Not long after what happened—the rape— he disappeared. No one really knows what happened to him."

Jerome sat there, his brow furrowed. "What about his parents? Did they live in town?"

Rachael gave a big sigh. "I guess we have to tell you everything." She got up, poured water into the big teapot and set up cups for us all.

"My grandmother's name was Jenny. She ran away from her husband who was beating her up and hid in a fisherman's camp upriver from the mill." She paused to pour the tea into our cups, and then continued with her story, our story.

Jerome kept looking from one of us to the other, then to his clenched hands, then to Rachael, then to me. He'd ask a question now and then. We told him everything.

"We didn't tell you not because we were trying to keep secrets from you, but because we just didn't want to hurt you. We didn't want you to feel any different than anyone else in the family, or in the town. We think we're good people. Jenny, Lily, Harry and Matilda were good people, and so are you. We can't help how other people judge us, but we didn't want you to grow up with any imagined taint that would make you feel less than anyone else." I tried to explain why we'd kept the secret for so long.

"Well," Jerome began, "the cat's out of the bag. Someone told Steve." We both nodded in assent. "I'm not really angry with you, just surprised. This is all just such a surprise." He again looked from one of us to the other. "I probably would have done the same thing if I were you." He hesitated. "Maybe someday you can show me my other grandparents' graves?" Rachael nodded, and got up to start cooking. "I guess we're having a light supper tonight." As we stood up he came around the table and hugged us both. "I always knew something was odd. I mean, I remember living with the nuns and the other kids. I didn't think it was strange at the time. Then when I was four you got married. I sort of missed the nuns and the other kids at first, but I had better food and more freedom, and it was fun getting so much attention. I figured it out later, but then just thought maybe with Ma in college you couldn't get married right away. I love you. You are the best parents a guy could have."

Would Jerome feel angry once he had time to digest this? Would he rebel, or harbor resentment? Would he grow to hate Rachael and me? That past, that haunting thought of a traumatic conception— did it touch him in ways we'd never understand? How does one handle shocking news? After dinner that evening Jerome went to Emma's and spent hours there. Whatever passed between them we will never know, but he seemed to be stronger, happier, and if possible more comfortable with himself after that.

Chapter 58

Exploring

Days went by without any word from Steve. We were all discreetly asking friends and acquaintances if they'd seen him about, but Jerome seemed to be the family member looking hardest. He appeared to have more connections in town than we did. School had brought him into contact with a lot of students, their parents and teachers. He started asking questions around. The first place he went was the grocery store. They said they had seen Steve and George coming in now and then. They didn't buy much, mostly bread, hot dogs, cheese – the cheapest things they could get.

The next place he went was the package store. The owner had a lot to say about these kids, first that they had come in to buy cigarettes and he thought they had stolen a couple of small bottles while he was cashing them out. He thought he saw one of them stuff them a bottle into his pants. Then he saw them hanging around outside, trying to get some of the older kids to buy beer or liquor for them. Mostly the kids didn't, but once in a while they did, or at least that's what he thought. He even suspected them of giving a drunk some extra cash to buy for them.

Jerome asked people if they knew where they were staying. No one seemed to, but all said they would tell him if they heard anything.

When he came home and told us what he'd learned we called the police and told them. We tried to minimize the parts about the alcohol but they said they had heard similar stories, so there was no covering it up. They said they would watch for them, and hopefully stop them and scare them before they got into serious trouble.

One night, very late, the phone rang. I turned on the light and answered it. It was Steve. "I'm sorry. I know I'm bad. I can't help it." He was crying and sounded like he had been drinking. "I can't change. I guess I'm just bad. I don't know what else to do, or how else to be. I just want you to love me." He sobbed loudly.

"I'm so sorry. I don't know what came over me." I tried to apologize. "I hit you. I didn't mean to." I could hear him sob again. "We love you. Please come home." I begged.

"I CAN'T! Don't you understand? I CAN'T!" and he hung up.

Rachael rolled over and looked at me with a sad and frightened expression. "It was him, huh?" I just nodded and lay back down.

Two days later when Jerome went down to pick up some gasoline for the truck, he talked to the service station attendant, who told him Steve and George had been in and bought kerosene. When they left, he said, they went up the dirt road by the river, up Jenny's Way.

Jerome was now fairly sure he knew where Steve and George were living. When he came home and told me I decided to go up and see if he was right.

The fields that replaced the lake were now planted with corn, which flourished in the silted soil of the river bottom. The old fishermen's path that we used to take was totally overgrown and a new path the fishermen used followed the river edge closely. A farm road through the corn paralleled the river but farther in. I walked the dirt road until it turned away from the river and became a path rising up the hill to where the cottages were.

I had not been to the cottages in years. When I took the kids fishing we stayed close to the bridge, not going very far up the shore. The path had become overgrown, and tall trees sprouted where bushes once stood, but some spots were recognizable. Memories of my youth came flooding back, the fishing and swimming with my childhood buddies, now all adults with their own kids. I passed the ledge where I remembered sitting with Rachael, wanting to kiss her but too afraid to do it. I remembered Rachael looking up, her black lashes over promising dark eyes, her shining hair. All came flooding back to me, people and events I hadn't thought of in years: Lily, Jenny, the kind women of the camp. I remembered how Jenny sent me out to split wood, and the silly dancing around on the porch. How young we were. How innocent.

As I walked this path I had a totally different perspective on life, on how difficult it can be and how complex, how corrupting. Our son, my son, Steve is likely living up here. What would I find? No one was on the road. All was quiet but for the leaves fluttering in the gentle breeze and a few birds singing.

When I got to the end of the last field and started to climb the hill to the cottages, I noticed the first one on the left was leaning steeply to one side, windows broken, ready to collapse. I could see the next one, up the right fork. It looked like the only one that might be in livable condition. I stopped and took it in: some moss on the roof, but not too much, the windows almost intact, with only a crack in one pane. The porch, though settling, looked sound enough and was swept, and a thin wisp of smoke drifted from the small rough brick chimney.

I tried to decide what to do. There was no sound. To alert whoever might be inside, I started to make noise, cracking a couple sticks as I climbed the last few yards.

Someone inside moved and offered a tentative "Hello?"

It was a woman's voice. She stepped out onto the porch, broom in hand, shading her eyes from the brightness.

Sharon, older, stouter, more worn, but with a warm smile of recognition, greeted me.

Chapter 59

Old Friend

"John E., is that you? I can't believe my eyes! Wow, have you grown! You're a man now!" She reached out and gave me a long hug. "I almost didn't recognize you. What are you doing up here? I can't believe this. Come on in. I've got hot water on. We'll have some tea." She ran her sentences together, not waiting for me to answer. She seemed very pleased to see me.

"Gee, Sharon, I think I'm as surprised to see you as you are to see me," I said as I followed her into the cottage, now having to duck my head to go past the threshold. The place didn't look too bad after the almost twenty years of age and wear since I was last up here, but now I noticed more the sad shabbiness of it. "Tell me why you're here. When did you move back? I thought you married and moved away." It was my turn to ask all the questions.

"Oh, John E., it just didn't work out. I lived with him for a while. Hal. We did get married and I had his son, but you know, sooner or later someone was going to figure it out." She poured us both a cup of tea and brought down a jar of sugar and unscrewed the cap. "By the time the boy was going to school somebody in town had heard a rumor and was passing it around. Pretty soon there was not only some nasty gossip, but guys were saying things to Hal, and then a few of them made propositions to me. Hal couldn't take it, and things got ugly. I told him I was going to leave and he said, 'Go ahead, but don't think you're taking the boy.' So here I am. I've got a little cash, and two kids I don't know and I can't see either of them—one little sweetheart in the ground, the other my ex turned against me." Sharon's eyes started to well up.

"Oh geeze, Sharon, that's too bad." I felt for her. She'd had a hard life, and she was a good person. And it didn't seem fair. "It doesn't seem fair."

"You're damned right about that. I'm a good person. I never hurt nobody, never cheated nobody, never killed nobody." At that her eyes flashed to me and then down to her tea. "Sorry. I didn't mean…"

"That's okay, Sharon, I know what you mean. And you're right, you're a good woman."

"John E., I liked being in town with my husband, but I never forgot the fun times up here. And what I miss the most is the lake. Isn't it weird? Now it's just trees and a meadow all the way down to the river. I used to love to just run out the door and jump in for an early morning dip. Or sit on the porch and see people row by, or fish. There was a lot of action on that lake. It was always busy during the summer. I sure do miss that. Almost nobody wanders up here now." Sharon shook her head. "You know, I heard all the gossip from town. I heard about you marrying Rachael and living up at the farm. That's great. You were meant for each other and the good life you have together. And you have a couple of kids too, right?"

"Yes. As a matter of fact that's why I came up here today." I looked directly into her eyes.

"What? Why did you come up here?" She looked back at me, genuinely puzzled. She obviously didn't know who Steve was, or else he wasn't living here.

"One of my kids ran away recently and I heard he came up here."

Sharon looked hard at me, her eyes squinted, and then her hand went up to her mouth and she gasped. "Oh. Oh. OH! NOW I know why he looks so familiar! Steve? He's YOUR son? Holy cow! That lying little brat!" Each time she paused another level of understanding and significance passed across her features.

"He started coming up here with George. George had been coming up here and sleeping on the floor, bought a cheap roll-up mattress. I make him roll it up every morning and stuff it in there." She nodded towards the back of the room. "He said his mother was abusing him, and you know I have a soft heart for young boys. No hanky-panky. I just wanted to help him. Then, a few weeks ago, Steve comes up with him. Same thing—parents are abusing him. No, he said, you don't know them, gave me some name like White. He did have a bruise on his face, so I thought, well, I've got enough floor space. They would bring a few groceries. They had big dreams. They were going to fix up the cottage down below, live there and rent it as a fishing camp, maybe get a few girls to work for them. I'd talk to them about the old days, the fun we used to have up here." She added hot water to her tea. "Want a warm-up?" I nodded. "Well," she continued, "I've got a few old friends who got wind of my being back up here. I'm glad to have them. It's hard being up here alone without the other girls, without anyone. I can manage, but it's not easy. I wish I could get another girl to come up. I don't want to be back in business, I just want to live. Having the boys here kinda helped with the loneliness, and they CAN split wood, just like you used to."

"Well, I don't know what to do now," I said, inspecting the cracks in the cup Sharon gave me. "That Steve is just unmanageable, not like me or Rachael, or Jerome. We just don't know what to do with him. But I sure am glad I know where he is now. He didn't tell us. He just left us worrying. We heard they had been stealing liquor too. Have you seen them drinking?"

"Well, them little buggers, they sit out on the porch all night, they light the kerosene lantern and talk and laugh. It really does remind me of old times. But if they're drinking they're doing it after I go to sleep. Come to think of it, they sometimes do seem kind of logey in the morning. I just thought they'd stayed up too late."

I start to think out loud. "I just don't know what to do. I don't know if I want them to know I've been up here. I need to go home and talk to Rachael and tell her what's going on. Then we'll figure out what we'll do next. Anyway, where are they right now?"

"They went into town. I think one of them is working at the mill, mostly just janitorial type stuff. I think the other one is helping him, trying to get a position, something like moving cartons around. Not a regular job, but they give him a few bucks. I guess it could be worse." Sharon got up, opened the door and threw the dregs of her teacup out into the woods.

"You're right," I agreed. "It could be worse, much worse."

Now that I felt more relieved about Steve, I started to gossip. "Did you know that Lily and Emma moved down onto the farm with us? Matilda asked them when she was still alive and it worked out great for them and for us. They've helped a lot. Then Lily joined the convent. Can you believe it? But Emma lives up in the bungalow. She likes her solitude."

"Yes, I'd heard some of that. I felt bad for Emma when she lost Linda. They were so close. I'd heard they moved to the farm some time ago, and heard a little talk about Lily, but I don't know that much. Sorry about Matilda. I didn't know her, but I always heard good things about her from Jenny. And you lost Harry too, I heard." I thanked her and nodded.

"Well, you know what?" I was finishing up the cold tea. "I'd better get out of here before they get back." Sharon nodded, stood up and gave me another big hug. "I knew you kids would be good together." I could see her struggling with something she wanted to say. "What about your other boy? I heard Rachael had another boy…" Her voice trailed off.

"Jerome." Sharon's eyes widened slightly as I went on. "Yes, she had a son. We adopted him. He's pretty much grown up now too. He's become a fine man. We worried about him, but it seems that he's not given us as much trouble as Steve. Odd, isn't it?" She nodded.

"Well, I'm really glad to see you, John E."

"You know I feel the same, Sharon." As I went out onto the porch I turned. "Keep an eye on those boys. We'll figure out what to do with them."

"You know I will. I'll send you word by one of my friends if something comes up," she called after me. As I went down the path and turned to look back, she waved.

Chapter 60

The Plan

I walked briskly back down the path and the dirt road, watching and listening for anyone on the road coming back from town. To my relief, I didn't meet them.

At the dinner table I shared my news. "Thanks to Jerome, we've found the boys." All eyes turned to me, forks in mid-air. "They are up on Jenny's Way." Everyone looked at me eagerly. "They are all right. They even seem to have gotten some work. And Rachael, Emma, you won't believe this – they're staying with Sharon." Gasps all around. I smiled.

"You're kidding?" came from Rachael and Emma simultaneously.

As I told them the whole story, Jerome smiled and Jenny's head snapped from one of us to the other as we talked about the camp and about the boys. Everyone was relieved.

In bed that night Rachael started the discussion. "What should we do?"

"I'm not sure," I replied, shaking my head. "I don't think they're ready to come back. They've got their independence now. But I'm glad we know where they are. And I'm glad they seem to be acting a little responsibly. Maybe having a job is the best thing for Steve. But I'm worried about what he'll do with the money."

Rachael nodded, musing aloud, "He doesn't seem to have the farming bug that Jerome has, and maybe it wouldn't be good to have them both trying to farm together. Too much competition. Steve's always comparing himself to Jerome."

I had to agree. "But what can he do? Obviously he can't spend the rest of his life up at the camp. He does seem mechanically inclined. Maybe we can get them to take him on at the garage? Or maybe just let him get the job at the mill, and if we're lucky he'll meet a nice girl and settle down.

"It was really good to see Sharon." I wanted to tell Rachael more about our meeting. "If I had dreamt of a good outcome for Steve up at the camp, it wouldn't have been better than having her there watching over them. Now they've got some kind of independence that they seem to need, and also someone we can trust keeping her eye on them." It was dawning on me I was starting to include George when I talked about Steve. The same thought must have crossed Rachael's mind because she glanced at me and asked, "Them?"

"Yeah," I replied. "It sounds like George has had a pretty hard life."

I told her more about Sharon and the hard times she'd been having. We wondered why some people escaped from difficult, dangerous or nefarious circumstances relatively unscathed, while others seem to drag their pasts with them like Jacob Marley's chains.

I realize now that Matilda and Harry gave me a lot of independence. I could have been up to no good, but they trusted me, and now I would have to trust Steve. I would have to trust that he would apply some of the values we had tried to teach all the kids.

We started to hatch a plan to get Steve back home. It didn't all come together at once, but as the days went on it developed into a solid strategy. We'd get Sharon involved.

Chapter 61

Step 1

When I presented our thoughts to Sharon, she liked and agreed to most of them. We were hoping that as time went by she would see the merit of the full plan.

While the boys were at work I'd drive as far as I could down the dirt road, usually bringing eggs, milk, potatoes, onions and other basics that I knew would make life easier for Sharon and for all of them. She and I would sit and talk about the plan and then sometimes reminisce for a while. Sometimes Emma came with me to see Sharon. Their first meeting was emotional. I hadn't warned Sharon we were coming to visit her.

Emma climbed out of the truck and took one of the bags I was carrying up the path. I called out to let Sharon know I was there so she wouldn't be startled. She opened the door to watch us climb the path up the hill. Emma was behind me and Sharon was leaning to see if she could recognize who it was.

"Oh, OH! I can't believe my EYES!" Sharon exclaimed as Emma leaned out far enough to be seen. Sharon held the door wide so we could pass by her with our bundles and jugs. Emma put her bags down on the table by the window and turned to give Sharon a big bear hug.

"My, my, my! You can't imagine how good it is to see you!" Sharon just stood there in front of Emma, looking her over. "You look great. That farming life must be agreeing with you." Emma nodded. Before they could speak again Sharon turned to pour the inevitable water into the pot for tea. "You're going to stay for tea, right?" She didn't wait for a reply but went right into setting up the cups. "Sit down, sit down." And while we sat she thanked us for the food and asked if we wanted any money for it. Of course not, I told her. Most of it was produce from the farm so it didn't cost us anything. As she unpacked the bags she exclaimed at each item. Oh, the eggs, oh, the milk and oh, OH, the cookies! "Rachael made them for you," I told her, and we sat down to tea and cookies.

Emma got up and walked around the room, looking closely at everything. She looked at the stove, which was Jenny's old one, moved down to this cottage. She stepped behind the blanket partition, asking, "Do you mind if I just peek into your room?" Sharon told her to go right ahead.

Emma came out with a red nose and eyes looking moist. Sharon nodded. "This used to be your cottage, wasn't it? Yours and Linda's. Does it look much different?" Emma shook her head. "I bet it has a lot of memories," Sharon said, and Emma nodded.

"It's odd. So much is still here," Emma began. "When too many mosquitoes were coming in Linda stuffed a little piece of rag into the hole in the screen. It's still there, can you believe it? I used to lie on the bed and look at the ceiling. A couple of nails came through and made a pattern that looked like a spider to me, and if I woke early and couldn't go back to sleep I would stare at them until they almost started to move. And there's a little heart that Linda carved into the woodwork, right there." She went to point it out, running her fingers over it. "What time does. How we lose people and yet still go on." She came back to us and sat down. "Strange, isn't it? They're gone, and yet not gone, and as long as any of us who can remember them are alive, they're sort of alive too, don't you think?" We both nodded in assent. "Well, sorry, I know that's not why we came here." And our conversation moved on.

"Hey, could you two wait here for a minute?" Sharon was on her feet. "I've got to put this milk down in the river or it will turn." She took the two gallon jugs by their handles. "Here, let me help you." Emma got up and took one and they both went down the hill. They were back shortly, laughing and panting. "Goodness," Sharon chuckled, "I remember when we could run up that hill, and I'd have a fella chasing me." And they both laughed some more.

We all sat down and Sharon told us how the boys were doing. "They're still working. I think the supervisors are happy with them and are glad to get the help, but they're getting paid under the table. I think gradually they'll actually take them on, if they keep their noses clean." Sharon poured more tea. "They're still liking it up here. It's still fun. Steve has even found somebody's old pole and they go down fishing. They're not half bad either – brought back a couple of good-sized brookies a few days ago."

"Well, it's good to hear that something he learned from me stuck." My voice had a little note of satisfaction.

"I'm trying to get them diverted from the drinking, like you suggested." Sharon went on, "I told them they should work on that first cottage down there, that they had some good ideas for it. Well, they went down to the store, picked up a couple of hammers and nails and a hank of heavy rope, and they started working on it. They tied the rope to a couple of the studs and they're trying to straighten it up. They're not the best carpenters, but they're at least trying. Did you notice it on the way up?" We both shook our heads no. "Well, come on down and see what they've done." We all went out and walked down the path.

They had tied thick ropes to some of the exposed studs and to nearby trees and were trying to bring the frame of the cottage back to vertical. They actually had gotten it to move about five inches. Another couple of inches and it would be almost plumb. I stepped inside and shoved it a little. "Tighten that up a bit, can you, Emma?" And Emma untied and tightened the ropes. "They shouldn't have much more to get it upright now. They're doing pretty good. Did they tell you what they would do next?"

Sharon said they were planning to bring some lumber home with them, from wooden crates the mill threw out. They wanted to use the pieces for braces, so that once they got it straight it would stay that way. After that they were going to try to figure out how to put some roofing on. The leaks were making the whole structure rot more. I told her to suggest tar paper. It wasn't too expensive, and wasn't permanent.

We talked a while longer and then Emma and I left, satisfied, so far, that our plans were progressing.

Chapter 62

Step 2

We continued to visit the camp and bring groceries. The cottage the boys were working on was starting to look almost usable. They had gotten a roll of tar paper and covered the roof with it, tacking it down with roofing nails and then using a little tar to cover the seams and nail heads. Now the roof wouldn't leak. With the leftovers they tar-papered two of the outside walls. That was wise because now you couldn't see through the cracks, and the wind and rain wouldn't come in either. They'd picked up a couple of mismatched windows. One they were able to nail up and the other leaned against the front of the house, too big to fit. The next thing they needed to do was make a door. That was fairly easy. The old hinges were still on the old jamb, rusty but usable.

I was impressed to see how far they had gotten. They were sweeping it out and using a couple of cartons as seats, and an old metal barrel with a board across the top served as a table. Several candles and a worn deck of cards sat on the table alongside two jars.

Sharon said she didn't think they were drinking anymore. They stayed up late working on the cottage and then unrolled their thin mattresses on her "kitchen" floor and fell asleep.

By the end of their third week of work the cottage was looking serviceable, a rough and ugly little shack but more or less wind and watertight. Now we just had to wait for foul weather. Autumn was early and winter was coming. The boys had been looking for a stove and found a small rusted pot-bellied one someone had left out by the roadside. Together they carried it back, stopping every fifty feet or so to rest. Sharon said they were sore for several days after that. They cut a hole in the roof for the stovepipe, and used flattened cans as flashing around the hole. They put bricks under the whole thing, with a couple extras under the edge of the stove where one of the legs was missing.

Sharon said the first time they tried to fire it up she thought they would burn the place down. They started it using twigs and it smoked so much they ran out coughing. Once they got it going they over-filled it, and she thought the place would go up in flames. Finally they got the drift of how to regulate it by closing the draft and using smaller pieces of wood. They got an old pot somewhere and an old aluminum coffee percolator and were able to brew up their own tea and coffee. Sharon got a kick out of them. She said it was like watching kids play house. They'd pick up someone's cast-off at the side of the road and bring it back and make it usable— a three legged chair, a washtub with a hole in it, a couple planks on cinderblocks where they unrolled their thin mattresses.

I thought that Steve was showing the first signs of maturity I'd seen in him, working towards a goal, thinking through problems. He showed more initiative on this cottage-building than he ever had at the farm. And that little one-room shack was neater than his room ever was.

Sharon still cooked for them most of the time. Nothing fancy: soups, hot dogs, and fish if they caught them. They'd sit at her cottage around the small table by the window, eating and talking. Sometimes Steve would talk about the farm. She thought he was getting nostalgic and making it sound like it wasn't such a bad place to be. He never said what farm it was that he came from, nor did he dwell on why he left. George on the other hand had nothing good to say about his family life.

One time the boys invited her to their cottage for tea, and they made a big deal of having a stained but clean cloth on their table and some bent spoons and chipped china cups. They all made a show of having tea, even pulling out a box of stale graham crackers.

They were getting more settled in, more comfortable, as the cold nights began to freeze the puddles and edges of the river.

We were ready for our next step in the plan.

Chapter 63

Step 3

Rachael and I woke up one morning to find the ground covered with snow. Jerome shoveled a path out to the barn and the chickens so we could milk the cows and get eggs. I shoveled the front walk and put the plow on the truck to plow up to Emma's. Rachael went off to school.

In the afternoon I drove up to the camp but didn't plow. Footprints coming down through the glistening snow signaled that the boys had walked to work that morning. Sharon made tracks in the snow on the way to the truck. She'd left a note for the boys saying she'd slipped in the snow and hurt herself, and she was going to stay with a friend who had come up to check on her. She said she'd be staying until she could walk better, and not to worry about her.

We drove back through the snow to the farm.

I waited a couple days to go back up there after another snowfall. Now there were new tracks in fresh snow upon the older indentations of previous snows. The boys were still walking back and forth. When I got up to the cottages I noticed it looked like they were going to Sharon's cottage to forage for food, and maybe sleeping there. The pile of wood on the porch was going down and would last maybe a week with these cold nights. The water in the barrel on the porch was frozen solid. For water they would have to melt snow; the river was now too treacherous to try to get water there. Living rough up in the camp was going to get harder. The narrow path they had tamped in the snow might keep them somewhat dry, but after they walked a mile to the camp their pants legs would probably be wet and they would be cold. A warm house and roaring fire with a hot dinner would be welcome. But they would be coming back to a cold stove they'd have to get stoked and then they would have to cook up something simple for dinner. We imagined them making hot dog soup with maybe some macaroni thrown in.

Rachael was getting tired of our plan. She was worried for her boy. Jerome and Sharon and I agreed that he could always walk into town. It wasn't as though he were at the North Pole. If he wanted to and was desperate enough he could come home.

Again we made some changes at the farm. Jerome moved out to the bungalow. He had finally started to date and he was seeing Nancy, one of the neighbor's girls. She was a nice quiet girl and they were dreaming of a future for themselves.

Emma, after years of being alone, agreed to move back to the house. She took the boys' room upstairs. She made herself a little corner reading area with a light and bookshelf and was able to get away to it when she needed to.

Sharon, who liked her independence, was realizing that it was just too hard to be up at the camp in the winter, and after a little pleading on our part agreed to stay with us at least until spring, although we were urging her to stay longer. She did say she worried about her "friends." She shared the boys' old room with Emma, both agreeing that it was big enough, especially since Sharon, more gregarious than Emma, didn't spend that much time in it.

We were just waiting for one more good snow before we made our move to get the boys back home. We hoped Steve would move into his old room, with or without George.

We didn't have to wait long for another storm. It came on a Wednesday night. On Thursday and Friday the boys had to walk through it to work and then back to the cottage. It was very cold that Friday night. We hoped that by Saturday they would be ready.

On Saturday morning, with Rachael, Jenny and Sharon in the truck, I plowed slowly up the dirt road to the base of the camp. The path was tamped down a little and a tiny plume of smoke came from

Sharon's cottage. Rachael had not been up here in years. It was a homecoming for her, and she quietly took it all in. Jenny had never been up here. This was where, we explained, her mother and grandmother had grown up, and where her great-grandmother for whom she was named had lived. It brought back so many memories to Rachael, as it had to me the first time I'd been back. For Jenny it looked – well, she said, like a poor shack.

Sharon got out and started up the path. The boys peeked out, having heard the plow come up the road. They came out on the porch to greet Sharon, both bundled in layers of clothes and looking cold. Sharon went inside, and in a minute Steve's head poked out. The rest of us got out and started up the path. Steve just stood there, watching us. Jenny ran up first, threw herself into his arms and gave him a hug. Rachael came up behind her and hugged Steve with Jenny sandwiched between them. Steve started to cry. I stepped onto the porch and hugged them all too. At this point Jenny wriggled out and ran inside calling to Sharon. We all were emotional.

"I'm sorry." Both Steve and I said it at the same moment. Rachael said how much she missed him, and he nodded. "Me too. I missed you too."

"Would you come home with us, son?" I asked in a gentle, hopeful tone. Steve turned to look at the door. "George can come too," I said. His head snapped back and he searched my face. "He can come? You've known about this for a while, haven't you?" I nodded.

We all went inside, where it was barely warmer than it was outside. There was no wood left on the porch and Sharon said she was relieved that they weren't burning the table or chairs to keep warm. They had a pile of branches by the stove that they had been trying to stoke the fire with. Steve told George that he was thinking about moving back to the farm, and paused to let George take that in. Then he said George was welcome too. George looked at him, then searched our faces. He had the look of a dog that had been kicked too often. We all looked back with tentative smiles and what we hoped were welcoming countenances. He nodded slightly, raised his shoulders and said okay, maybe he'd try it for a while.

Chapter 64

Home

Sharon checked the cottage and made sure any loose food was put into tins or thrown out. Otherwise, she said, the mice would have invaded it, eaten everything, nested in the linens and left little "presents."

The boys went down to their cottage and grabbed what few treasures they had managed to collect. Steve had purchased a small wind-up alarm clock that he tucked into his jacket. George had a worn copy of a Jules Verne novel and a compass. They latched Sharon's door, and their own. I had been putting the truck in the barn so there would be no snow in its bed. The boys jumped into it and the rest of us squeezed into the front. We turned around and drove slowly back down the dirt road, Jenny kneeling backwards on the seat between us watching out the window as the boys waved wistfully back at the cottage they had spent so much time working on.

We were so hopeful our plans would work. We had rearranged Steve's old room with two single beds just in case George decided to come too. We didn't change much else. We left the comic book covers Steve had tacked on the wall along with some of the drawings he had done.

We came home to a warm kitchen full of the blessed aroma of a chicken dinner Emma was preparing. The boys looked dreamily around the kitchen. We shooed them into their "new room" and told them to change clothes and take a bath. They said they hadn't had a bath in a month and were overjoyed at the prospect of hot water.

Steve sat in the kitchen with us having coffee while George took the first turn in the tub. Everyone was bustling about the kitchen, helping Emma with the final preparations, when Jerome came in from the barn, a ten-gallon milk jug in each hand, his large frame filling the kitchen doorway. He took it all in, Steve looking grubby and the rest of us excited and in a festive mood. We all held our breath in anticipation as a look passed between the two brothers. Emma was the only one who didn't notice, continuing to stir a pot noisily.

Steve raised his voice loud enough to be heard above the noise. "I am so sorry," he began, and all of us exhaled and looked from Jerome back to him. "I am so sorry about all the things I said. I didn't mean them." All of us except Jerome went over to him and hugged him and told him how much we loved him and that it was okay. As we went on with our work, pausing to look at him when we could, he continued, "I didn't mean to make you worry. Well, maybe at first I did, but then I felt bad about it. I just wanted you to love me as much as everyone else. How stupid." Jenny sat down at the table with him and fiddled with the silverware next to her plate.

"It wasn't stupid," she said with gravity, shaking her head. "You were sad because you thought we didn't love you."

"I was so wrong," Steve replied to Jenny. "When George told me how mean his mother was, I began to realize what a good family I had." He swallowed hard, looking intently at his coffee cup.

"I don't care about all that stuff. You're home now, and I'm glad." Jenny smiled at Steve and he smiled back.

Jerome walked across the room and held out his hand. Steve took it and Jerome pulled him close and hugged him. "I hope you don't do that again. You had ma and pa really worried, and me chasing you all over town." I could see Steve's eyes shining.

"I know now I am the luckiest guy..." Steve trailed off. He sat back down and concentrated on the coffee grounds at the bottom of his cup, shaking his head.

Then, as I turned from the stove and brought the bowl of mashed potatoes over to the table, he said, "I like working at the mill. Do you suppose I can keep working there?"

I searched his face and replied, "Sure, if that's what you want to do." A look of relief passed over him, and he let out a sigh.

Rachael and I had talked about this, and we thought it was good for him. We hoped to instill our value of thriftiness and help him get a savings account. "Want to go to the bank on Monday and open up an account, so maybe you can save some of your earnings?"

He smiled and replied, "That would be great."

George came into the room, clean with just-combed hair. He spoke softly. "THAT was wonderful. Your turn, Steve." He was bringing his dirty clothes into their new room when Rachael stopped him. He said without hesitation, "I can wash them. I wash my clothes all the time." A look passed among the rest of us in the kitchen.

Jerome said, "Oh boy, this is setting a bad precedent." We all laughed.

Rachael said he could leave them in the basket by the back door, and that Emma and Jenny usually did the laundry but he could help if he wanted.

George was nervous, polite, and awkward. We had him sit at the table as we put the food out and waited for Steve. Jenny talked to him, asking him about the cottage he and Steve had worked on together, and about school, and fishing. We determined that Steve and George had been in the same class at school and they were both close to completing their studies.

We were sitting down to dinner when Steve came down. Having shaved the thin layer of new hair from his chin he looked more like a man than ever before. We started the discussion that we knew might send them back to the wild.

I began. "We are so happy to have you back with us, Steve, and we're happy that you're with us too, George." Both of them looked expectantly at me. "I know this is not what you want to hear, but you should get your high school diplomas. Both of you." They looked at me and then at each other. "Your mother and I have looked into this, and you can take classes after you get out of work," I continued. "And you could complete them and get your diplomas in six months." Again they look at me and then at each other. "And, you won't have to see your old classmates. It's only older kids and adults who take these courses, people just like you. There is no shame in it." I looked hopefully at them both, waiting for a sign from them. Steve looked at me, then at George. He nodded his head slightly. Then George nodded his. Then they nodded more vigorously. Rachael sighed in relief. Everyone smiled.

Chapter 65

More Secrets

The evening after the boys' arrival back home, Steve took me aside. He invited me into his bedroom on the pretext of showing me a book he'd borrowed, but closed the door behind me. George was sitting in the corner, away from the lamplight so that I could barely see him.

"Dad," Steve began, "didn't you think it was strange that I knew so much about the family?" I nodded, waiting for him to go on. "It was George's dad. He told him everything." Steve turned to look at George.

And then George started talking. He had a soft and hesitant voice. "My dad left my mom when I was little. He was a drinker and she was mean. Well, they were both drinkers, but I was stuck with her. He used to go up to Jenny's Way, just like lots of the guys from the mills. He had a liking for Lily. Well, he got to know most of the goings-on up at the camp—who favored who, who was on the outs, who got pregnant and how. I only know this because in the last few years before he died, I would sneak off to be with him when my mother went on a bender and I was afraid she would beat me up. Dad wasn't much better, but his liver was getting bad so he had to lay off the booze some. I'd run over to his place, which was above the market. It wasn't much of an apartment, but he'd make me something hot, even if it was only oatmeal. He'd feed me and I'd be safe. So in those last years we got kinda close. He'd ramble on about the camp and about how it was the one time and place in his life where he felt happy." George coughed, and Steve asked him if he was okay.

I wasn't sure what this was leading to. "Are you sure you want to talk about this now?" George nodded. "Yeah, I think you need to know. Anyway, he said that he couldn't figure out why you didn't try to kill that Kevin yourself." He paused to look at me and I had to squint to see his expression. "Dad also said that Lily had gotten hooked up with some rich guy from up on the hill who promised to marry her. My dad was sad about that because he liked Lily, but that slick character knew how to talk his way into her heart. Then she got pregnant and that's how Rachael came along." He paused again, looking fearfully at me. "I'm sorry, Mr. Black. I don't mean to insult you, it's just what my dad said. I don't even know if it's all true."

"That's okay, George. What else did he say?" I'd had inklings of this but no confirmation until now, and I was interested in hearing it all.

"Well, he talked about all the people up at the camp, but mostly about Lily, who he loved. But he said she had a religious bent he thought was silly—I mean she was, you know, a prostitute. He couldn't understand it, but he tried to court her. When she wouldn't have him he married my mother, who made them both miserable. Nobody liked the Hunts. Buck, Kevin, Lucille—they were just a sad lot. He said that when Rachael was attacked by Kevin and the fellas got together…" I nodded. "My father was one of them. He said they had a pact never to talk about it, but he told me they went after him. My dad couldn't understand why you didn't get all up in arms like the other guys. I mean, she was your girl." He raised his shoulders and put his hands palms up as though trying to make sense of it. "Anyway, they got that Kevin. He said they took care of him. And every time we talked about it he got a gleam in his eye. So, why didn't you go after Kevin?" I could see him looking up at me from under the hair that was hanging into his eyes.

"Kevin disappeared. There was nothing I could do, and Rachael needed me." I started to explain, looking at both George and Steve. "I was crazy with anger, at Kevin and at Rachael for not letting me walk her home. It was the only time I ever raised my voice to Harry. I think we were both surprised. But Harry, ever the wise one, sat me down and told me that all the anger and hate would never change what had happened. He said it would only hurt me, and the best thing I could do now, the very best thing, would be to help Rachael because she was going to need me. Rachael needed someone to talk to if I had courage enough to just listen. She told me about that night, about Kevin disappearing, about the nuns planning to send her to college, and then, that she was pregnant." I looked down at my hands. "It was my test. She needed to know if I would stand by her or leave. I passed the test." I looked at Steve. "And you need to know I love you, but that I love Jerome just as much as the rest of you kids. I felt so bad about hitting you, but it seemed cruel to throw that in his face." Steve nodded back at me and let out a big sigh "I know. I was feeling neglected. But after being at George's house with his crazy mother and hiding out at the camp, I realized how much you cared. I was wishing and praying that you would find us up at the camp."

I looked at both of them. "This has been a hard time for us all, but I'm glad you're home, both of you. And George," I said, looking at him, "you're welcome here. You have nothing to fear from this family." I could see his eyes well up under the hair hanging into them. He sniffed and wiped his nose on his sleeve. "Here, use my handkerchief." I pulled it out of my pocket and went over to hand it to him, but George had already pulled something from his pocket, a tightly folded handkerchief, and started to untie it to reveal something within.

"My dad gave this to me. It's only brought us bad luck, so I thought I should give it to you." He said this as he was unfolding the carefully wrapped item. He rolled it onto the bed, seeming almost afraid to touch it. A jackknife. He nudged it towards me. I picked it up and examined it. It was medium-sized, good quality. I turned it over and engraved on it was the inscription "Kevin, from Dad." I actually dropped it back onto the bed. But, realizing that any power it might have had came full circle and now might bring more healing to our little clan, I picked it up and handed it to George. "Here. You boys give it to Jerome. I think it was his father's, and I think he would appreciate it." George took it reluctantly, carefully wrapping it back into the handkerchief.

I leaned over and hugged them both.

Chapter 66

Resolution

The next day Jerome came out to the barn while I was milking. He pulled up a stool and waited for me to finish before he started to talk.

"The boys gave this to me. You know about it, don't you?" Jerome pulled out the pocket knife and opened his hand to show it to me. I nodded. He cleared his throat and hesitated. "There's something I need to tell you." I looked up at him. He was very serious. I nodded. "Something I never told you, never told anyone…" I just waited for him to continue. "When I was a teenager, still in high school, Steve was in grammar school and we'd meet at the bottom of the hill to walk home. Well, a man started approaching me on the way home before I met up with Steve. He was drinking sometimes, I think. He'd follow me for a little way and try to talk to me, try to be friendly. He was in a wheelchair. I was frightened by this guy. He was deformed and creepy. But for a couple of weeks he'd try to talk to me. He knew my name. He offered to buy me dinner, and he said he wanted to be friends." Jerome hesitated and I just watched him. He seemed to get more anxious as I waited.

"Who was it? Did he try to do something to you?" I wanted to help him get this out. He shook his head.

Jerome stood and put the knife on the stool he'd been sitting on. "No, he was in a wheelchair. I could have always run away from him. It wasn't that kind of threat, it was something else, like he knew me, and that was scary." I nodded. "Well, after a couple of weeks, I thought maybe we should talk, have dinner or something. So when he met me on my way home I picked up a couple of sandwiches at the diner and we went up and sat on one of the benches overlooking the dam. No one was there. I didn't really want to have people see us. I'm not sure why I was so cautious—I must have had a premonition." He paused and I nodded again. "So we sat down to have the sandwiches and he pulled out a bottle and every bite of the sandwich he washed down with liquor." Jerome crossed his arms. "When he finished, he told me. He told me who he was. He said, and I remember every word, 'Do you know who I am? I'm your father, Kevin Hunt. I'm your damned father.' I was shocked. He was so creepy and he even grabbed my arm." Jerome put his hands behind his head and leaned back, looking up towards the barn's loft. Then he dropped his hands to his side, clenching and unclenching his fists. "He started to cry, and talked about how sorry he was, how he ruined everyone's life, how he'd tried to change."

"Jerome," I tried to interrupt. "No, no, don't interrupt me. I have to tell you this. I have to tell someone. I can't stand it anymore." I stopped and just watched my boy who was so anxiously trying to finish his story.

"I killed him." Jerome's eyes were big and he held his shaking hands palms up in front of me. "He kept going on about how he'd tried to change, about how sorry he was and about how proud he was of me. He was agitated, taking a swig from the bottle, rolling the wheelchair back and forth in front of me. Then he grabbed my arm again and I pushed him away. I didn't want him touching me. He rolled backwards, swinging his arms like he was losing his balance, almost like he was flying. He hit his head really hard on the railing. The wheelchair collapsed and he and the bottle and the wheelchair went under the railing into the lake. It was very deep there before the dam went out. I rushed over and looked down into the water after him. I didn't see him. He was gone. I didn't know what to do. Should I go after him, try to save him? If I did, could I have gotten him up? How would I get him out of the water? I knew there is no easy way to get out from there—it's just steep concrete sides. All these thoughts rushed through my mind as I looked down at the spot where he disappeared. Then bubbles came up and I knew I'd hesitated too long."

I stood up and reached for him, but he pushed me away. "I killed him," he repeated in a defeated voice.

"No. It was an accident." I reached for him again and hugged him, this boy as tall as myself with tears in his eyes. "It was an accident."

I wanted to comfort him but didn't know where to start. I stood there looking at him, trying to absorb this news. A million things rushed through my mind. When did this happen? Why didn't we notice Jerome was having trouble or that he was upset one day when he came home from school?

It seemed like he could read my thoughts. "I met Steve. I was a little late. Once in a while I was late and he'd wait by the corner store for me. I knew I had to act normal. I tried to put the whole thing out of my mind so that I wouldn't give any clue to Steve. By the time we got home I was just being myself, but I thought about it at night and went over and over it. Finally I went to Emma and asked her about the camp, and in a week of talking she told me a number of secrets about the camp that our family never talked about. She told me about Buck and Rachael and Kevin. I knew, but I couldn't tell you, and she asked me not to let you know that she'd said anything. So when Steve said what he did, and you and mom talked to me, it just confirmed what I'd already known."

I stood there in front of this boy who was wise beyond his years. What should I do? Should I tell him he should have jumped in and tried to save Kevin? Should I tell him he could have told us? No, he'd been through enough.

"I feel bad that you had to carry this burden by yourself for so long," was my response.

He searched my face and looked relieved.

"No more secrets?" I ventured. He shook his head. "Good," I said. "We've had enough drama for a lifetime."

Chapter 67

Finish

Steve and George did get their high school diplomas. They worked on machinery around the farm and on the truck and on a car they bought together, then on their friends' cars. They continued to work at the mill until they saved enough money to open up a little garage, a tiny one-bay garage, but gradually they built it into a reasonably thriving little business, adding on several bays after a year. They saved enough to be able to buy the house next to the garage and they moved in there. Neither of them married.

Jerome did marry that sweet little neighbor girl, Nancy, and she moved into the bungalow with him, that bungalow that had seen three generations of my family conceived. They have a little girl, a tot with flaming red hair, and another baby on the way. Jerome secretly told me he is hoping for a boy. They talked about it, and if it's a boy they want to name him Harry. With Jerome and Nancy's help, the farm is thriving. No one seemed to know that Kevin had come back or the he was in the mud where the lake had once been. Jerome kept the knife and always had it in his pocket.

Emma moved into Steve and George's old room, happy to have her own space again and more room for her books. She still trudges back and forth to the library, but Steve bought her a rolling cart to put her books in and she says she never felt so spoiled, rolling the cart up and down the hill. She's come out of her shell a little and even joined the library committee, helping them with fundraisers and special events. She met a widow on the committee and they have become fast friends.

Sharon moved out to be with one of her "friends" who still worked at the mill. By now she has moved back and forth several times. We tell her the room is always open, and she is glad we allow her that and don't try to influence her too much. We just call her our gypsy, and she loves it, saying she's never been good at staying put.

Jenny has the boys in a roil. Everywhere she goes heads turn and eyes follow her. She looks the image of her mother. Thankfully she's bright and cautious. She knows how to flirt, but also how to be serious. She knows her mind and is more attracted to the sounder, smarter boys, not to the flashier more clever ones. Matilda instilled some amazing values into that girl.

Rachael and I agree – we think we are the luckiest couple in the town and have the best children. Rachael, with little grey hairs appearing at her temples, looks even more beautiful than in her youth. She still has her dark eyes, her graceful walk and her gentle demeanor. She is still my one and only love.

Epilogue

We all still make annual trips up to Jenny's Way. Sometimes we camp out. Sometimes we fish and eat and play cards. We start a fire in the rusted old stove and make our cups of tea and reminisce. This rough little camp that brought us all together is our common history. It unites our odd clan of related and unrelated folks searching for the bond of family. I've decided that Jenny's Way was more than just a path to the camp. It was a way of life, a way to treat those people who need our help. Jenny's, like Matilda's, was a place where people were welcome and could find comfort and help, and so we carried on her tradition at the farm, and our children carry it on too. They forged a bond here at Jenny's Way, and we will carry the memory of the people and the place. We'll share the tales, and they will grow, even after all the shacks are crumbled and the stove a heap of rust.

Pictures from the real Jenny's Way

Addendum

Photo by Dennis Delaney, courtesy of the Sprague Historical Society.

Research shows that eleven cottages, built by villagers as weekend getaways, once stood on the shores of a small lake created by a mill dam on the Shetucket River in Baltic, Connecticut. Legend has it that at one point women may have lived in some of these cottages and "entertained" mill boys there, although no firm evidence of this has been found. The real road to the camp was called Ginny's Lane and descended from the farm on Pautipaug Hill Road in Baltic, not far out of town. The dam, pictured on the postcard above, was just upriver from the bridge on the current Route 97. Today only a few large berms mark its former location, but the Veterans Memorial still exists on the south side of the river where the boardinghouse and men's club once stood. Although the road now running through the cornfields by the river is on private property, fishing along the river below the high-water mark is allowed and said to be very good. With permission from the property owners, you can still find the layers of freshwater clam shells up on the hills along what was once the pond's shoreline. To find out more

about the cottages, the mills and the history of Sprague and its villages contact the Sprague Historical Society:
HistoricalSociety@CTSprague.org.

Map

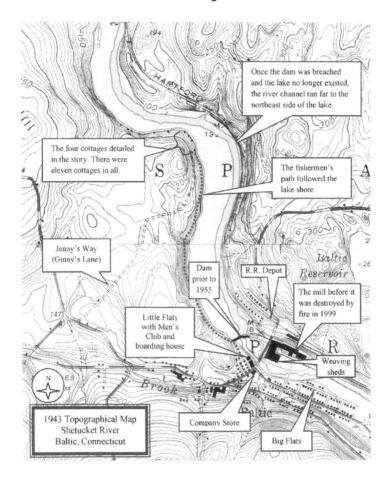

The Old Mill

The old Baltic cotton mill was built on the Shetucket River in 1899 (after another burned down). A rebuilt mill operated until 1967. It burned in 1999, leaving only a granite shell, which was subsequently torn down.

New England, with its abundance of water, hilly terrain and river valleys, was a perfect spot for mills powered by water before newer forms of energy (steam, diesel, electricity) allowed manufacturing to relocate. Mill towns were historically the backbone of the industrial revolution in New England. Now their productivity and influx of capital has retreated to other parts of the country and the world, leaving the old towns to fall into disrepair. With the efforts of local citizens many of these towns are now enjoying a renaissance.

Jenny's Way is the second in Diana's
Shetucket River Milltown Series.

As stated in the disclaimer, all characters and their exploits are fictitious.

Made in the USA
Lexington, KY
07 July 2013